TRUE BLUE MURDER

ELISE M. STONE

True Blue Murder
Copyright © 2016 Elise M. Stone

Cover designed by Susan Coils

Quotations from Shakespeare's works are taken from http://www.opensourceshakespeare.org/

Published by Civano Press
Tucson, AZ

ISBN 978-0-9888482-6-9

CHAPTER ONE

Lilliana Wentworth pushed the cart with the wobbly wheel toward the dining room of the Rainbow Ranch Retirement Community. Or, as most of the residents referred to it in private, "the old folks home." She wrestled the contrary cart, which carried her plants on the top shelf and her equipment bag on the bottom, past the poster board sign announcing the First Annual African Violet Club Show and Sale. Fighting the cart's threat to tip over, she turned into the large room that had been transformed from dining facility to exhibit hall by moving the tables into two neat rows, one on each side, with a large space in the middle. Several members of the club, already at their assigned places, busily tended their plants.

It took her only a minute to find the table with a little gold stand holding a place card with her name on it. She was at the far end of the room, but that was all right with her. It was better than being in the middle, where the judges would have already seen so many gorgeous plants they all seemed to look alike. If you couldn't be first, when they were eager to start their evaluations, last was almost as good, when their memory of what they'd seen was fresh as they finished the judging.

She meticulously positioned her violets, a dozen of her best, then added the snack-sized plastic bags holding leaves she would sell to the visitors, their stems carefully swathed in moist cotton. The leaves were very popular at sales, since almost everyone could afford a dollar. Buyers scooped them up with fanciful hopes of having their own blossom-covered plants in a few weeks. And selling them gave Lilliana a little extra to spend on her African violet addiction. She would also sell the mature plants, the best ones commanding a price quite a lot more than a dollar.

Except the True Blue hybrid. That one was her treasure, and hopefully, the one that would win Best in Show. She'd created it herself, a lush Saintpaulia with blossoms of deep purple bordering on midnight blue. She loved blue and had been trying for two years to breed a plant that would bloom in her favorite color. It was almost impossible to get a true blue. When she'd woken up one morning and seen the flowers this plant produced, she'd clapped her hands and gasped. She might have shrieked, but a retired librarian had a bit more decorum than that. The burgeoning blue blooms where only green leaves had grown the night before seemed almost magical.

She picked up the makeup brush she used for grooming and started flicking bits of dirt from the leaves. Appearance was everything when it came to being judged in a show. She'd snipped all the less-than-perfect leaves from her plants before loading them on the cart this morning, but the bumpy ride down had left a few leaves with specks of vermiculite and soil. When the plants were clean, she stood back and evaluated the positioning, deciding to nudge one a couple of millimeters farther back so it was perfectly aligned with the others.

"Lily!" a hearty male voice called out.

"Good morning, Leonard." As usual, Leonard was looking healthier than any seventy-four-year-old had a right to. An engineer before he retired, since moving to Rainbow Ranch he'd committed to being a tennis pro. Lilliana had yet to go to the exercise room and not find him there. Unless he was out on one of the two tennis courts the facility had built, giving lessons when he could find someone to take them, smashing serves over the net when he couldn't. As a result, his body reminded Lilliana of Arnold Schwarzenegger in his prime, or possibly Jack LaLanne, the fitness guru who had performed amazing feats well into his nineties.

Leonard put the box he was carrying on the table next to Lilliana's. "I see we're neighbors." He peered over at her African violets with a look on his face that said he was beating the judges to their job. "Nice plants this year. Especially that blue one."

The warm glow Lilliana felt at his admiration for her baby made her decide Leonard wasn't as insufferable as she'd thought he was. "Thank you." She took a look at the plants Leonard was lifting from the box and arranging in his spot. "That yellow one is pretty. Kind of a golden color, isn't it?"

A smile spread over Leonard's face. He squared up his shoulders and ran a hand over his bald head, preening at the compliment. "It did turn out nicely, didn't it?"

"Did you create that variety?" She tried to sound casual, but she was anxious about her competition for best new hybrid. Some of the club members had a lot more experience than she did. And, like in figure skating, judges of African violets could be swayed by their familiarity with the contestant almost as much as the expertise. Oh, not in a show that took place under the African Violet Society of America rules. In one of those, plants were carefully anonymous to prevent any kind of favoritism. But Rainbow Ranch was an informal club, not nearly large enough to form an official chapter of the AVSA.

Leonard waved a hand. "Oh, no. I tried breeding hybrids a couple of years back, but I didn't have the patience to make sure they didn't get contaminated by neighboring plants. No, I bought this beauty from Rob's Violet Barn as a Christmas present to myself."

Feeling slightly ashamed of herself, Lilliana relaxed a bit. "Well, I'd better put this cart back in the storage room so someone else can find it if they need it."

Leonard nodded. "You do that. I'll keep an eye on your plants."

Lilliana's eyes widened as she wondered why they would need watching with only the members of the club in the room. Did Leonard know something she didn't? She wasn't sure, but she decided not to dawdle on her errand and get back to her African violets as soon as possible.

Most of the exhibit spots were now filled with gorgeous flowering displays. Growers usually specialized in one thing, either a type of plant or a color or something, because there were just too many kinds to grow them all. She passed Mary Boyle's display of semi-miniatures in cute little ceramic pots. They were so sweet, somewhat like Mary herself, who looked up from her chair with a smile as Lilliana passed by. Mary gave Lilliana a thumbs-up. "We got this one covered, right?

"Definitely." It was easy for Lilliana to be gracious to Mary, since she knew they were competing in different categories. As a matter of fact, no one else grew semi-miniature plants as far as she remembered, so it was a good bet Mary would win a blue ribbon.

Frank Bellandini rushed up to Lilliana's side and clutched her arm. Behind lenses as thick as glass architectural blocks, his eyes bulged so hugely they looked as if they might fall out of their sockets and tumble onto the floor. "You'd better watch out for Bette Tesselink. She stole my red hybrid and is claiming it's hers."

Lilliana sighed. Bette was a pain in the behind, if she did say so herself. The woman was always causing trouble in one way or another. "Did you tell the judges?"

"Of course I did," Frank said. The more he spoke, the redder his face got. "They asked me if I had any proof. Proof? I wasn't taking pictures with my cell phone when she stole it."

Lilliana stifled a smile. Frank had one of those basic cell phones for the elderly, the ones with the large numbers and minimal functionality. She wondered if he realized his phone didn't have a camera. "How do you think she managed to steal your cultivar?"

"Remember that meeting when we all brought in the hybrids we were growing and talked about how we'd gone about creating them?"

She nodded her head. Her seeds had barely sprouted, with four little leaves peeking out from the stem in the small plastic cup. She'd been a bit embarrassed to show it to the others, whose plants had been much further along. But she thought she could use advice in raising the hybrid for the show, so she'd brought it anyway. When Frank suggested snipping off a damaged leaf, it felt like cutting off her arm, but she did it.

"Well, she must have taken a cutting off one of my plants then. No one but me has a red like that," Frank said.

Lilliana thought that would be hard to prove, but she remembered being impressed by the deep crimson Frank had achieved. More than impressed. She'd been terribly jealous.

Lilliana glanced at the clock on the wall to see what time it was. Ten minutes remained before the show officially opened, but the hallway was already filling up with people waiting to get in. "I'm sorry, Frank. Maybe the judges will take that into account when they come to your plant."

"They'd better." Frank glowered, and his face, which had almost returned to its normal color, turned so red Lilliana hoped his blood pressure was under control.

"I should put this cart away before they start letting people in," Lilliana said. "Good luck to you, Frank."

"And to you, Lilliana." Frank headed across the room to his assigned table.

Lilliana continued pushing the balky cart. As she drew closer to the door, she saw the dreaded Bette Tesselink at the first table on the left, right next to the entrance. Oddly for Arizona, she wore a dark blue dress instead of casual clothes. Perhaps she felt the show required more formal apparel. Bette's mouth was much too large for her face. It looked even larger as she bared her teeth in what, for her, passed for a smile.

"Lilliana," Bette said. "All ready for the competition?" Bette lifted a pot containing an African violet covered in lovely yellow blooms from a cardboard box and put it on her table.

"As ready as I'll ever be. And you?" Her gaze went to Bette's display and was immediately drawn to a lush hybrid with deep crimson blossoms. Frank was right. There was no doubt in her mind that "Bette's" plant had been grown from a leaf of Frank's spectacular hybrid.

Bette pulled her last plant from the box, an intense blue violet labeled Deep Blue Sea. The same deep blue as the one sitting proudly at the center of Lilliana's own display. The pressure in her head built until she thought it might explode. Blood sang in her ears. "What do you think you're doing?"

Bette feigned innocence as her eyes widened to match the size of her mouth. "Why, whatever do you mean?"

Lilliana stuck out a trembling finger and pointed at the blue flowers. "That's my plant." Her voice was tight and louder than she'd intended.

"It seems to be on my table." Bette stared past Lilliana, as if looking at something across the room.

"But you stole it from me." Lots of eyes had turned toward the two women, including those of some of the waiting visitors.

A beefy man dressed in a suit rushed over to them and held a finger to his lips. "Please keep your voices down, ladies. This is an important event for Rainbow Ranch, and we don't want to spoil it for people."

Lilliana turned to face Dale Ackerman, mayor of Rainbow Ranch. The overpowering scent of his aftershave forced her to take a step back before speaking. "I don't think our guests want a cheater in the show. This woman stole my plant."

"I'm sure all of this can be worked out to everyone's satisfaction," Mayor Ackerman said. "I'll have a word with the judges. Meanwhile, it's almost time for us to open the doors, so could you please take your places."

Lilliana thought about arguing the point, but it was useless to talk to the mayor about an African violet problem. That was a decision for the judges, and she intended to have a conversation with them when they got to her table to evaluate her True Blue hybrid. Meanwhile, she was still standing with the cart in front of her. She took a deep breath and forced her hunched shoulders to relax as she exhaled. She nodded, fighting to control the fury she felt as Bette's face turned smug. If the woman thought she'd won the battle, she was seriously mistaken.

Lilliana pushed the cart out the door and toward the back of the building, where there was a TV room on one side and a storage room on the other. Even through the closed door to the TV room she could hear the sound. One of the residents with a hearing problem—probably Wayne Victorsson, who was always misplacing his hearing aids—had turned up the volume again.

She opened the door to the storage room and pushed the cart through. Shelves along one wall held cartons of toilet paper and tissues, boxes of holiday decorations, and office supplies. The astringent smell of cleaning chemicals coming from the adjoining housekeeping closet prickled her nose. She removed her equipment bag from the lower shelf in case anyone else needed to use the cart. Her plan was to head over to the baseball field at the elementary school between the closing of the show and dinner. Lilliana was an outdoorsy person, used to being active, and knew that spending the day inside would need to be offset by exercise.

She hitched up her slacks, which had slipped down from her

waist, and thought they seemed looser than the last time she'd worn them. Had she lost more weight? She'd have to stop by the clinic one day next week and get on the scale. As much as she liked exercise, she wasn't all that fond of eating. After over seventy years of three meals a day, she'd tried just about everything, and it all tasted pretty much the same now.

Being careful to close the storage room door behind her, Lilliana hurried back to the dining room. People were already filing in as she took her place. She fixed a smile on her face as a woman trailing two young children stepped up to her table and peered at the leaves.

"Can you really grow a plant from one of these?" She pushed a stray strand of hair back from her face, then made a quick grab for the little boy, who had reached out to touch one of the plants the minute she let go of his hand.

"Of course you can. African violets are easy to grow from leaves. If you take one over to the education table," she paused and pointed across the room to the table directly opposite hers, "they can pot up the leaf for you and tell you how to care for it."

The woman looked doubtful, with a touch of longing in her eyes. "I really like that dark purple one," she said, looking at the True Blue.

"So do I." Lilliana smiled. "That's one I bred myself. I only have a few leaves of that one, but I'd be happy to sell you one." She picked up one of the plastic bags and held it out to the woman.

The doubt on the young woman's face changed to determination. "I'll take it." She let go of the little boy again to get her wallet out of her purse, and the boy promptly stuck his hand out to stroke the leaves on a variegated pink Saintpaulia.

"It's fuzzy, Mommy." He looked up at his mother with wide brown eyes.

"Don't touch the plants, Jimmy." She turned to Lilliana and handed her the dollar. "I'm sorry."

"It's not a problem," Lilliana replied, while gritting her teeth and being grateful he hadn't touched the True Blue. She took the dollar bill and put it in an envelope.

The woman headed in the direction of the education table with Jimmy tugging on the bag with the leaf inside, trying to take it out of her hand. Lilliana silently wished the potting people luck with keeping Jimmy out of the tub of soil.

It looked as if the entire village of Rainbow Ranch had turned out to see the show. Not that that was surprising. In a town of five hundred souls, not counting the approximately eighty residents of the retirement community, not much happened for entertainment.

Even Theodore Pulaski, owner of Pulaski's Gourmet Grocery, had shown up. Older than most of the retirement home's residents, Mr. Pulaski was still spry and active in his ninth decade. Lilliana might have lost her appetite for regular meals, but Pulaski's Gourmet Grocery carried an excellent assortment of chocolates right next to the cash register, and Lilliana had felt obligated to sample one of every variety. In fact, she was considering doing a second sampling, just to be sure of which kind she liked best.

"Good afternoon, Mrs. Wentworth," Pulaski said as he stepped up to her table. Dressed in a gray plaid western-style shirt, he stood a few inches taller than Lilliana's own 5'10". Just tall enough for her to look up at him. "Mighty nice flowers you've got here."

Lilliana found herself blushing. *How ridiculous!* "Who's minding the store today, Mr. Pulaski?"

"I decided to close, in honor of the event, you know." He slowly looked around the room. "And, judging from how crowded it is in here, it doesn't look like anyone would be at the store anyway."

"I think you're right." Not sure what to say, but not wanting Mr. Pulaski to leave her table quickly, Lilliana asked, "Are you interested in African violets?"

"I like all things from nature. I've never paid attention to African violets, though. Pretty little plants, aren't they?"

"Yes, they are. Would you like to grow one of your own?" She wasn't sure whether she was more interested in the money from a sale or in offering to mentor the grocer in how to grow one.

Pulaski looked surprised, as if he hadn't considered the idea before. "You know, Martha was the one who took care of the houseplants. After she passed, I could never keep them alive. One by one, they all shriveled up on me. I think I have a black thumb."

"Oh, nonsense. It's just a matter of the right amount of water and light. I could help you with that."

His bushy eyebrows raised slightly, then lowered. "Well, I might just give it a try then. Only I'd better start with something that already has a head start. Is that one for sale?" He pointed at one of the two Ionanthas on the table.

Lilliana breathed out a breath in relief. She'd been afraid he'd ask for the True Blue, and she hadn't wanted to turn him down. The Ionantha was a species plant, often called the original African violet because it grew natively in, of course, Africa. Not at all rare. A smile spread across her face. "Yes, it is. Only, since I'm having that one judged, you'll have to wait until tomorrow evening to pick it up. Or I could bring it to the store on Monday."

"I'll be happy to come back for it tomorrow. How much do I owe you?"

CHAPTER TWO

Lilliana's pulse rate doubled as the two judges who had come out from Tucson, the Rainbow Ranch club not having anyone qualified for judging yet, approached her table. She took one last look at her plants and resisted reaching out to turn a pot just a little. The action might signal to the judges she was trying to hide some imperfection, and that was the last thing she wanted to do.

She recognized Joan MacLeod, a petite woman whose most noticeable physical trait was her dark auburn hair, cut in a short style with bangs, the ends of her hair spiking out around her chin. The man beside her wasn't familiar.

"Hello, Lilliana," Joan said. "Have you met Jim Thompson?" Her gaze flicked toward the man before coming back to Lilliana.

Lilliana extended her hand. "No, I don't believe I have."

The young man, who reminded her of a college professor, looked down his nose at the proffered hand as if debating whether he might catch something unmentionable from touching it, then slowly raised his hand to meet hers. After barely brushing fingers with Lilliana, he mumbled, "Pleased to meet you."

Joan shuffled the papers from the clipboard she held and eventually pulled out three sheets and put them at the top of the stack. She clipped them in place and said, "You have entries in three categories: Standard, Species, and New Hybrid. Is that correct?"

Lilliana nodded. "Before you begin—" she swallowed hard "—I want to mention that I believe Bette Tesselink may have violated the rules."

"Oh?" The college professor sniffed.

Lilliana looked in his direction. No sympathy there. She concentrated on Joan. "You may have noticed that Mrs. Tesselink is showing a plant identical to my True Blue violet." She pointed, unnecessarily, at the plant in the middle of her table. "This is a hybrid I created totally on my own from violets in my collection. I believe that she, um, *took* a leaf from this plant at one of our club meetings and is claiming it as her own."

"Do you have evidence of when you created this particular hybrid? Or when this alleged theft took place?" Joan asked, not unsympathetically.

Lilliana thought back to the log she kept on all her plants—the dates repotted, fertilized, which shelf and type of light it was growing under—that was down the hall in her apartment. "Not with me," she began, "but I could get my log for you."

"I don't think we have time to wait." Thompson glanced in the direction of the entrance, where Russell Ellison, the owner of the Rainbow Ranch Retirement Community, was coming in, along with a reporter from a Tucson television station. A man carrying a camera on his shoulder followed behind.

Lilliana opened her mouth to speak, but realized she wasn't going to win this debate at the moment, and the last thing she wanted to do was draw the attention of the television reporter. She could just imagine everyone in town pointing fingers at their TV screens as she argued that her plant had been stolen. She'd forever be known as the crabby old lady from the African violet show.

As the judges worked down the checklists and whispered between themselves while examining her entries, Lilliana was drawn to the exchange between Ellison and the reporter.

Ellison, a middle-aged man with a mustache and goatee, perhaps in compensation for the lack of hair on his head, raised his arms expansively, taking in the whole room. "As you can see, Biff, Rainbow Ranch Retirement Community has many events and activities for its residents. We believe seniors have plenty of life left in them and assure that every resident has activities that will keep them interested and happy. This show is just the first of many similar events we have planned for the coming year."

Lilliana couldn't believe her ears. When the committee from the African Violet Club, of which she was chair, had approached him about holding the show on the premises, he'd been adamant about *not* having it. He objected to the extra work involved for the staff, the potential liability of having the general public onsite, and a million other things. It had taken many reassurances, and the purchase of liability insurance for the event by the club, to convince him to allow it to take place at all. Now he was taking credit for organizing the show.

"The show continues through tomorrow, and we hope lots of people will make the easy drive from Benson and Tucson to check it out. While they're here, we'd be happy to give them a tour of our facilities and tell them about all the opportunities and amenities at Rainbow Ranch for both active adults and those requiring more personalized care." Ellison turned an ingratiating smile toward the camera.

Ah, that explained it. Ellison was hoping to capitalize on their work and sell his retirement home to more people. As best Lilliana could recall, there were at least ten apartments and several casitas still vacant. Not too far northeast of Benson, Rainbow Ranch had to be a good seventy miles from Tucson. While Benson had a small hospital, Ellison had underestimated the desire of the elderly to be closer to the world class facilities in Tucson. Thus the vacancies.

"Thank you, Lilliana. Your entries this year are very nice." Joan turned and headed toward the judges' table at the end of the room between the two rows of show plant exhibitors. Thompson followed her.

Lilliana had almost forgotten about the judging while watching Ellison's antics with the reporter. She had worked so hard to develop her hybrid and was hoping for a ribbon. To be honest, she wanted the blue ribbon, first prize, but she would understand if Frank took that one for his crimson beauty. She'd be happy as long as the winner wasn't Bette Tesselink. She could only hope the judges would realize she had told the truth about Bette.

While waiting for their decision, she bent over to straighten the display of leaves to give herself something to do. And felt her pants slipping down again. She stuck a thumb in the waistband to pull them up and wished she had worn a belt.

The room was still full of visitors. Lilliana hadn't realized there were quite so many people in the small town of Rainbow Ranch. Or maybe people had come out from Benson to see what was going on. From what she could see through the windows at the end of the room, it was a beautiful day for a drive. Clear blue skies, cloudless, the way they would be until the summer monsoons, with a bright sun warming the desert air to a temperature in the low seventies by the afternoon. Perhaps the snowbirds, refugees from Minnesota winters, had been drawn out as well on this glorious March day.

Lilliana turned her head toward the squeaking sound approaching her table and saw Mary Boyle pushing her walker down the row.

"Would you like to get some lunch?" Mary asked. Mary's graying hair, which had started the day in a short, curly style, had escaped the bonds of hairspray, with several strands sticking out at odd angles.

Lilliana glanced toward the judges' table.

Mary, noticing the direction of her gaze, said, "Don't you worry. I already checked. The judges won't be announcing the winners until after one. They're serving a lovely buffet out on the patio."

She really wasn't hungry, but the hopeful look on Mary's face begged for company.

"You go on," Leonard chimed in. "I'll keep an eye on things for you. Then you can watch my table while I grab some food later."

"All right," Lilliana said as she came out from behind the display table. "Lead on, Macduff."

Mary turned her walker around and started pushing it toward the exit. Lilliana followed with mincing steps, containing her usually long stride to match Mary's shorter one.

When they reached the patio, Lilliana confirmed she had been right about the weather. Although the chill of winter lingered in the light breeze, the air was very pleasant when the wind went still.

Shall I compare thee to a summer's day? Thou art more lovely and more temperate.

With the show and sale occupying the dining room—one of Russell Ellison's objections to having it—the facility had been forced to find an alternate venue in which to serve meals. The poolside patio was perfect for lunch, but it would be too cool in the evening to be comfortable. If Lilliana remembered correctly, dinner would be delivered on trays to the individual apartments. A buffet breakfast would be set up in the lobby tomorrow morning.

"Let's take a look at what our choices are." Mary directed her walker toward the buffet tables set up on one side, where a line was already forming. Of the dozen round tables on the patio, half were filled with diners. Although only slightly past noon, it appeared as if most of the residents had already eaten. A large contingent seemed to be of the early-to-bed-early-to-rise faction, and meals were often the highlight of their day.

As they got to the start of the food tables, Mary reached for a tray and then hesitated as she realized there was no way for her to carry it while pushing her walker. Noticing Mary's dilemma, Lilliana said, "Why don't you tell me what you'd like, and I'll put it on a plate on my tray for you."

"Thank you, Lilliana. I always forget I can't do some of the things I used to." A wave of sadness crossed Mary's face and settled in her eyes before she banished it and continued, "But there are always good people like you to help me when I need it."

Lilliana wasn't sure what to say to that. She didn't feel particularly good. It was common decency to help another human being. She felt fortunate to be healthy and agile. Of course, she worked at that, but that didn't necessarily guarantee a person wouldn't develop problems as they aged.

She thought back to the house in Tucson she'd shared with Charles for a decade. If it hadn't been for the stroke, they'd be there still. But afterwards he was never quite the same. He certainly couldn't keep up with the yard work or the little repairs around the house. Moving to Rainbow Ranch, where all that was taken care of, along with weekly housekeeping services and twenty-four hour medical care, had seemed like the right thing to do.

"What about some of the chicken salad?" she asked Mary.

Once their plates were filled, Lilliana looked around for a table. None were empty, but she saw one where Frank sat with Nancy Gardner. She headed in their direction.

"Mind if we join you?" she asked.

"Not at all," Nancy said. "I was just telling Frank how nice it was to be eating outside today. All we needed to make it perfect would be to have our friends join us."

Friends? Lilliana had barely met Nancy. She wasn't a member of the club nor on the softball team Lilliana was trying to organize. She seemed to remember her from the one early morning tai chi class she'd gone to. One because posing on the grass around the gazebo like some oriental geisha wasn't her cup of tea. She much preferred a brisk walk.

Lilliana put the two plates of food, napkins, and utensils on the table, then looked for a place to put the used tray. Ah, they'd set up another table with plastic bins for dirty plates and trays not too far from where the group was sitting. By the time she returned to the table, Mary had seated herself next to Nancy and was digging into her plate piled high with potato salad, pickles, and a buttered roll along with the chicken salad. Lilliana split her own roll with her knife and proceeded to fill it with the scoop of chicken salad she'd taken.

"See, I told you." Nancy was pointing a finger at Lilliana's plate.

Lilliana scrutinized her dish, wondering what Nancy thought was wrong.

Frank responded, "You can't judge by Lilliana. I don't think I've ever seen her eat dessert."

She looked from Frank to Nancy and back again, her brow furrowed with confusion.

Seeing her expression, Frank said, "Nancy was telling me she doesn't think they serve very good desserts here. Nancy bakes some interesting recipes." He accented the word interesting, and Lilliana wondered exactly what he meant by it.

Nancy provided some enlightenment. "If they'd serve my peach pie seasoned with chili powder, I'm sure lots of people would take dessert. Everything here is so bland."

Peach pie with chili? Lilliana wasn't sure she'd eat that combination. Ever.

"Well, lots of folks here are on bland diets," Mary said, echoing what Lilliana had been thinking. "What with ulcers and different medications, they have to be careful with what they serve. Otherwise, people might get sick."

"I'm sure they wouldn't get sick from my pie," Nancy insisted. "I'm going to bake one tomorrow. I'll bring it down here so everyone can sample it. Then you'll see."

Lilliana made a mental note to skip dessert again tomorrow.

Frank tactfully changed the subject. "I saw you talking to the judges. I suggested they might want to disqualify Bette Tesselink."

"I said something similar, but they didn't seem to believe me." Lilliana stopped and remembered the judges' comment. "I might just go back to my apartment and get my log to show them after I finish eating."

"I had mine." Frank looked glum. "They said that wasn't good enough. It's my word against Bette's. I suppose it would be the same with yours."

"But that's not fair," Lilliana said. "Did they even question Bette?"

"Not to my knowledge," Frank said. "She turned on the charm, telling Jim Thompson how she'd read about his prize collection in the Arizona Daily Star and saying she'd like to talk to him privately about his techniques. Obviously buttering him up, hoping it would sway his opinion."

Lilliana sighed. "Well, hopefully Joan will see through her. She's been judging shows for a long time, and I'm sure she's run into Bette's kind of shenanigans before."

Frank looked up at the sky as if imploring a higher power. "We can only hope."

Lilliana sneaked a glance at her watch. It was five after one. "Shouldn't we be getting back? I don't want to miss the announcement of the awards."

Frank took his cell phone out of his pocket and checked the time. "You're right."

Mary gazed regretfully at the potato salad remaining on her plate, then pulled a plastic sandwich bag from her purse. She spooned the remainder into the bag, zipped it up, and put the bag back where it had come from before rising from her chair. Lilliana gathered the plates and utensils to put on the clearing table on their way out. It was hard for her to match Mary's slow progress. Everything in her wanted to run back to the show room and get the results. Her heart was tripping rapidly as she imagined walking up to accept the blue ribbon.

CHAPTER THREE

Someone had set up a microphone in front of the judges' table and, not unexpectedly, Russell Ellison was positioned very close to it. He looked over his shoulder toward the judges as he straightened his tie. Joan McLeod and Jim Thompson had their heads bent together, almost touching, as they whispered to one another and tapped their pencils on the clip-boarded sheets in front of them. In a moment of decision, Joan assertively wrote something next to three of the entries, then raised her head and nodded at Ellison.

He thumped on the microphone to make sure it was live, then said, "Ladies and gentlemen."

The visitors quieted and turned their attention away from the displays. Most of them started to gather in the open space between the tables. The club members tensely waited at their positions for the results. Mary stroked the side of one her tiny pots. Frank straightened his pile of business cards. Lilliana flicked a spot of soil from a leaf. The only one who didn't seem tense was Bette. She stood calmly behind her table checking her lipstick in a compact mirror.

Ellison cleared his throat. "Ladies and gentlemen," he repeated. "I am pleased to announce that the judges have made their decisions. In the category of best species plant, third place goes to Sarah Higgins."

Sarah, a nondescript woman in her early eighties and president of the African Violet Club, hurried, in a relative sense, up to the judges' table and accepted the yellow ribbon from Mr. Ellison with trembling fingers. When Lilliana first joined the club, Sarah had taken almost every blue ribbon in the shows she entered. However, it was more difficult for her now since she'd developed Parkinson's disease. She had good days and bad days. On the bad days, she often forgot about tending to her plants. On the good days, the tremors made it difficult for her to do the delicate work of trimming and potting them. Lilliana wasn't looking forward to the next ten years. You never knew what infirmity would sneak up on you once you reached a certain age.

Sarah wobbled back to her table between Bette and Frank on the opposite side of the room.

"And, for second place in the best species plant category, Lilliana Wentworth."

Surprised for a moment, Lilliana almost forgot to retrieve her red ribbon. She'd been so focused on the hybrid category, she'd forgotten she was an entrant in the species category as well. She accepted the ribbon with a mumbled, "Thank you" and quickly went back to her table.

"And the first place ribbon for best species plant goes to…" Ellison paused for dramatic effect. "Leonard Rothenberg!"

Lenny's face lit up like a kid at Christmas. Lilliana was happy for him. While not the most expert grower, Lenny was an enthusiastic one. And he was one of the few members of the club capable of lifting things when they needed things lifted.

The editor of the Rainbow Ranch Gazette was snapping pictures with a digital camera. Lilliana hadn't seen him come in. What was his name again? Sam something. She was having such trouble remembering names lately. Horn. Sam Horn, that was it. He'd been to the retirement home before to write articles for his six-page weekly newspaper. He usually called her after a softball game—when she could field two teams—to find out the score and who won for the sports page. The show would probably take up a full page of those six this week. That reminded her...

She scanned the room and finally spotted the television cameraman off to the side, camera perched on his hip and the film—or tape, she supposed—rolling. Biff Buckley, the reporter, seemed to have disappeared. This didn't surprise Lilliana. In fact, she was amazed he'd stuck around as long as he did. Covering a tiny flower show at a remote retirement community wasn't exactly a plum assignment.

Ellison picked up another blue ribbon from the judges' table. "In the category of semi-miniature plants, first prize goes to Mary Boyle."

Mary reached up to her head as if to straighten her hair, but all she did was succeed in putting more of the gray-streaked locks askew. She rose heavily and maneuvered her walker into position as the crowd applauded. And kept applauding as she made her way to the front of the room, albeit with waning enthusiasm. By the time she reached the front and accepted her ribbon, only two people were clapping. The applause picked up again as she turned and headed back to her table but didn't last long. It was replaced by the shushing of her walker over the carpet and the intermittent squeaking of the wheels. The shuffling of feet as the crowd waited for her to get back to her place. Someone coughed.

Ellison turned back to the judges and picked up the last sheet of paper with the prize winners' scores. "And now," he said, turning back to the mic, "in the prestigious category of best original hybrid, third place goes to Pieter Joncker for his beautiful variegated"—Ellison pronounced it 'varagated'—"blushing pink violet."

More applause. Lilliana had passed Pieter's table several times today, but she hadn't realized he had a hybrid entered as well. That decreased her chances, but she still felt that the real contest was between herself and Frank. Her breath came in rapid, shallow pants, and she forced herself to breathe slowly and deeply.

After Pieter returned to his table, Ellison continued. "The second place ribbon goes to Frank Bellandini for his Criminally Red hybrid. A fitting match to the color of the ribbon," Ellison quipped.

Lilliana's heart was racing. Could she really have won first place with her first attempt? It seemed to take hours for Frank to walk to the microphone and accept his red ribbon. Hours with her pulse pumping in her ears. Her hands fluttered over her plants, briefly brushing the petals of the True Blue African violet.

Ellison picked up the last ribbon on the table, the first place blue for best hybrid. "And the first place ribbon for best original hybrid goes to—" Another dramatic pause.

Lilliana could barely stand the suspense.

"Bette Tesselink for Deep Blue Sea."

The crowd erupted in appreciative applause as Bette attempted to float up to the mic like a queen. Given her bulk, the queen would have been Victoria and floating was out of the question. The outsiders clapped, but not the members of the African Violet Club. Most of them were looking at Lilliana with sympathy in their eyes.

She couldn't believe it. How could they award the ribbon to Bette when she'd told them Bette had cheated? The new judge might have been swayed to believe her, but surely Joan knew better. Lilliana looked down at her True Blue violet and felt tears welling in her eyes. She blinked quickly to clear them.

"Now, if all the blue ribbon winners would meet with me in front of the building, Biff would like to interview you for the late evening newscast." Ellison stepped away from the mic and headed toward the entrance where Biff Buckley had magically reappeared, just in time to get in front of the camera again. Once Ellison reached him, the two of them turned toward the front door, most of the crowd trailing behind to watch—and possibly appear in—the television interview.

"Tough luck, Lily," Lenny said.

"There was no luck about it." Her mouth tasted bitter, filled with the acridness of alum. Her eyes met Leonard's. "She cheated. She cheated both me and Frank. If I didn't win the blue ribbon, Frank certainly should have."

"Maybe it's something we could take up at the next meeting," Lenny said.

"Perhaps," Lilliana said. Then her eyes narrowed. "And maybe it's something I can take up right now."

Lilliana marched off in the direction of the judges' table where the two Tucsonans were gathering up their papers and packing them into briefcases. She had to try one more time. "Joan, could I have a word with you?"

Joan looked as if she were about to protest, then turned to Jim and said, "Why don't you take these things out to the car. I'll catch up with you in a minute."

As soon as Jim stepped out of earshot, Joan said, "What is it Lilliana? We already discussed your objection to Bette's plant and decided we had to accept her word on the fact she bred her Deep Blue Sea cultivar."

"But what if I brought you my plant log, showed you how I pollinated the mother plant, the dates I planted the seeds, and how I made sure they were from my own hybrid seeds? It would just take a minute to get it from my apartment."

Joan sighed. "Frank had his log with him. As did Bette. Without evidence to the contrary, we have to accept that Bette's log is as valid as Frank's—or yours. And, in our determination, Bette's hybrid was the best entry."

"But you know Bette Tesselink," she pleaded. "Has she ever developed a hybrid of her own before, much less two of prize-winning quality?"

"The case is closed, Lilliana." With that, she firmly closed her briefcase, punctuating her remark. "And now I have to meet Jim at the car. It's a long drive back to Tucson."

Lilliana watched in frustration as Joan hurriedly left the room. There must be something she could do. She wasn't the kind of person to take things lying down. She'd go on the Internet, check the AVSA rules for showing plants, even though the club didn't technically follow them. There must be some way of, if not winning the ribbon herself, at least taking it away from Bette.

As she turned back to her table, she noticed Sam Horn standing a few feet away, a thoughtful look on his face.

"Trouble in African violet paradise?" he asked.

"How long have you been standing there?" Lilliana asked. "I would have thought you'd be outside with the TV people getting the story for the Gazette."

"Oh, I have plenty of pictures for a story. Besides, it looks like there might be a better story in here."

Lilliana considered telling him all about it. The idea of Bette Tesselink being exposed in the Rainbow Ranch Gazette held some appeal. But claiming that Bette had stolen her plant, and thus the blue ribbon, would sound petty without a reversal of the decision by the judges to back up her story.

"No story," she said. "At least for now. I'll let you know if one develops."

Sam looked at her skeptically for a moment, then turned and left the room.

* * *

Most of the exhibitors had returned to their tables once the television people had gone. Mary wearily pushed her walker back to her place. Lilliana's heart went out to her. With all the excitement and stress involved, she wondered if Mary would be able to hold up for a second day.

Lilliana's pants had slid down on her hips again, and once again she reached under her blouse to hike them up. This time, she slid her thumb around to the front and found the cause of the problem: she'd lost the button. She scanned the floor around her feet, turning around to make sure it hadn't fallen down behind her.

"Lose something?" Leonard asked as he stopped rearranging his table to make room for his prize ribbon.

"My button. I've been wondering why my pants couldn't seem to stay up today." She glanced down at the floor again and wondered if it would be too lacking in decorum if she got down on her hands and knees to look under the table. Maybe not, since the tablecloth would hide her from the dwindling crowd in the center of the room, but there might be another problem. With the arthritis in her knees, getting up again might be an issue.

Lenny joined in the hunt by looking on the floor behind his own table. "Are you sure you lost it here?"

"No," Lilliana said. "As a matter of fact, it could have been anywhere from my bedroom to the patio outside." She sighed. "I suppose I'll just have to see if I have another one like it in my sewing box later. Meanwhile, I think I have a safety pin in my equipment bag. If you could watch my table again for a minute…"

"Not a problem," Lenny said and scanned the room. "It's not like there's a big crowd right now."

"Thanks so much," Lilliana said. "I'll only be a minute."

She hurried down the hall, anxious to get the safety pin and return to the show. She'd expected to find some of the crowd out here, but it appeared that after the award ceremony most had followed the television people out the door and not come back. The hall was empty except for the sound of an *I Love Lucy* rerun blaring from the entertainment room. Had Wayne been in there all day?

Lilliana shook her head. She'd go batty if she watched as

much television as some of the retirees. She'd much rather spend her time playing softball, walking around the grounds, and tending her African violets.

And there were always books. She loved books—mysteries, romance, adventure stories, poetry. New books and old classics. It was almost time for her annual reread of Shakespeare's plays, a summer tradition she'd started when she found children used the library a lot less often when school wasn't in session. She never tired of reading Shakespeare.

As she got to the end of the hall, she noticed that the door to the storeroom was open. She was sure she'd closed it when she left. With visitors from town—and out of town—she'd wanted to keep the honest people honest and not tempt them into stealing something by having it visible from the hallway. Who could have left it open?

She was sure it wasn't one of the housekeeping staff. At least, pretty sure. They all seemed conscientious and trustworthy. Maybe someone else had decided to put some personal belongings in the room during the show and neglected to close it behind him or her.

An odd smell came through the open door as Lilliana neared it. Not the odor of cleaning products she'd noticed before, but something fetid and foul. It reminded her of a not-very-clean public restroom. Strange. She hoped an animal hadn't gotten inside and marked its territory. If it had, she'd have to notify someone to come and clean it up. But, when she pushed open the door to allow her to enter, the room didn't contain an animal or its excrement.

On the floor, her deep blue dress pushed up above her chubby knees, was Bette Tesselink, a blossom of red spreading from the roots of her hair. Her body was twisted as if she'd tried to avoid the blow. And beside her, covered in blood, was Lilliana's softball bat.

For a moment, everything stopped. Lilliana couldn't take her eyes off the body, couldn't force herself to breathe. Even her heart stopped beating. At last she took a breath, and her heart resumed its tha-thump in her chest.

Lilliana kneeled next to the body, pushing the bat out of the way so she could feel for a pulse. She grasped Bette's wrist with bloodied fingers and watched her chest for the slightest rise and fall. Bette's chest didn't move. The skin underneath Lilliana's fingers was already beginning to cool. It was clear Bette Tesselink was dead.

"Is there a problem?" a familiar male voice asked behind her.

Lilliana turned and saw Russell Ellison standing in the doorway. His face paled as the blood drained from his cheeks. "Is she…?"

Lilliana nodded. "I'm afraid so," she said as she painfully got to her feet.

"What have you done?" Ellison's pallor had been replaced by shock and outrage.

"Done?" For a moment Lilliana was puzzled, until she realized what Ellison meant. He thought she had killed Bette. "I haven't done anything. I just found her here."

"Come out of there immediately," Ellison said, then glanced down the hall as if looking for someone or something. "Miguel," he called out, using the name of the facility's handyman, "call 9-1-1."

Ellison seemed flustered. Well, who wouldn't be, thought Lilliana. While this wasn't the first death at the Rainbow Ranch

Retirement Home, the others usually happened while the resident was in bed. A heart attack or stroke or just old age. Nothing of the magnitude of—she might as well use the word —murder.

Ellison kept glancing at her, then looking away when she noticed his stare, as if afraid she would grab the softball bat and bash his head in, too. There had been times she wanted to do that, but this wasn't one of them. She felt sick to her stomach, wondering who could have done such a thing. And why? Bette, while annoying, hadn't deserved to be murdered.

"Didn't I tell you to come out of there?" Ellison's voice rose in pitch. He was probably thinking that after engineering so much good publicity for the home, it would all be undone once news of the murder got out.

Lilliana took a few steps toward the door, noticing the murmur of conversation coming from the hallway. Apparently the news had already started to spread. By the time she reached the door, the hallway was filled with octogenarians trying to get closer to the doorway for a glimpse of the body.

CHAPTER FOUR

An interminable amount of time oozed by while waiting for the police. Lilliana was sure that once an experienced law enforcement officer arrived, Russell Ellison's ludicrous accusation would be seen for what it was.

Eventually muttering and shuffling and the sound of a man's voice saying "Excuse me. Clear a path, please" broke through the murmur of retellings and speculations. The crowd humped and swayed as the voice grew closer. The sea of humanity parted and revealed a young man in a blue police officer's uniform. Under the cap, his face was so dewy fresh Lilliana wasn't sure he was old enough to have graduated from high school.

"Good to see you, Chief Cartwright," Ellison said.

Chief? This boy was the chief of police? Lilliana hoped he had some experienced detectives working under him.

"We have a situation here," the retirement home owner said.

The boy's eyes bugged out as he stared at the body. "Is she dead?"

"Of course she's dead," Lilliana said.

The chief turned his attention to Lilliana. "Who are you?"

"My name is Lilliana Wentworth. I came here to get a safety pin from my bag and found Bette just as you see her now." Well, not quite the way she lay now, Lilliana remembered. She had moved the softball bat to check to see if Bette was alive. Then she'd lifted her wrist to take her pulse. She couldn't remember whether she'd replaced Bette's arm in the exact same position or not. Lilliana put her bloody hand behind her back.

Cartwright pulled a pad and pen from his shirt pocket and started making notes. "What time was this?"

"About fifteen minutes ago," Lilliana said.

"And I arrived here right after that," Ellison said. "It's a good thing, too. Otherwise Mrs. Wentworth might have gotten away with it."

Lilliana's head jerked up, and she gaped at Russ Ellison. "Get away with it?"

Ellison nodded. "It looks to me as if that baseball bat is the murder weapon." He tilted his head in the direction of the bat. "And who does the bat belong to?" His voice rose a major third on the last word and hung there.

"You know very well it's mine. I left my equipment bag in here before the show started. Anyone could have come in the storage room and taken it. The door is never locked."

"But you're the one with the motive," Ellison continued. "Why, you even spoke to me about Bette supposedly stealing your plant. I think that when she won first prize, you couldn't stand it any more and decided to take matters into your own hands."

"That's preposterous!" Lilliana couldn't believe this. Was she going to be railroaded before there was any investigation, any autopsy?

"Now just a minute." The chief's voice cracked as he attempted to assert his authority. Beads of sweat covered his forehead. "Can someone tell me what is going on here?"

Lilliana gave him the abbreviated version of what had transpired today, minimizing the argument and her feelings about Bette of course, then ending with, "Where's the crime scene unit? Don't they need to dust for fingerprints, gather the evidence?"

"Right," the chief said and pulled out his cell phone. He punched a few numbers and waited for an answer. "Uh, dispatch? This is Chief Cartwright in Rainbow Ranch. I'm going to need CSU out at the retirement home. And could the ME come, too?"

There was a pause as whoever was on the other end talked for a while.

"It appears we have a homicide," Chief Cartwright said. After another pause, he nodded his head and said, "Roger." He put his cell phone back in his pocket. After a minute, he gathered himself up and said, "I'd like everyone to go back in the dining room now while we wait for the auth—crime scene unit. I'll need statements from everyone."

Lilliana tapped him on the shoulder. "How long until they get here?"

"Who?"

Lilliana began to wonder if she was dealing with Barney Fife. Even her failing memory wasn't as bad as the chief's. "The ME and the crime scene unit." She was not entirely successful at keeping the exasperation out of her voice.

"Oh. About forty minutes."

"Forty minutes? Where in the world are they coming from?"

"Bisbee. The sheriff's office. Rainbow Ranch is too small to have its own crime scene unit."

Lilliana should have anticipated that. A town of five hundred people wouldn't have all the facilities of a city like Tucson. Or even Bisbee. "And how soon will the detective get here?"

"Detective?" Chief Cartwright's face scrunched up in puzzlement, then cleared as he realized what Lilliana meant. "Oh. There is no detective. I'm the only cop in town."

* * *

They'd hustled all the people who were either exhibitors at the show or visitors—those who had remained—into the television room. The fifty-inch flat screen was tuned to the Game Show Network. Thank goodness someone had turned down the sound. Of course, that made the answers shouted out by the captive audience more annoying.

The television room ran the length of the dining room wall and was set up like a home theater, only narrower. Ten rows of five chairs with an aisle down the side provided more than enough room for the potential suspects and witnesses. It wasn't used much, most residents preferring to watch television in the privacy of their own apartments, except for a few like Wayne who were too cheap—or couldn't afford—to have a television of their own. The exception was Saturday night when the facility supplied a DVD of a special movie they thought the residents would like to see. They even provided popcorn. No soda, though. Housekeeping had refused to deal with the sticky spilled liquid.

Lilliana fidgeted in her chair. Speaking of sticky residue, she really would like to wash Bette's blood off her hands, but the chief had been insistent that no one leave the room until the crime scene techs were done with them. Washing her hands wasn't the only reason she wanted to make a trip to the restroom. The iced tea she had with lunch had percolated through her system, and she wasn't sure how long she'd be able to wait. Obviously the chief had never dealt with a group of senior citizens and their need to use the restroom on a frequent basis.

Wayne's angry voice coming from the doorway behind her interrupted her ruminations. She turned around to see what was going on.

"You'd better let me out of here, or I'm going to pee all over your leg," Wayne said.

Miguel Ibarra, the retirement home's handyman, who had been pressed into service to guard the door, looked unhappy. The creases which outlined his mustache deepened as he frowned. "I'm sorry, señor. The chief of police says no one may leave the room."

Wayne raised his voice to a shout. "Then let the chief come in here, and I'll pee all over his leg!"

The sound of a zipper unzipping was clearly audible to Lilliana, and she wondered if Wayne was about to carry out his threat. She certainly could sympathize.

"Señor!" Miguel's eyes widened, and he reached out a hand to stop the elderly man from exposing himself and, worse, urinating in public. "Wait here, and I will get Chief Cartwright."

Wayne's face took on a self-satisfied expression.

Within seconds, Miguel was back with Cartwright, who

looked harried and flustered.

"What's this I hear?" Chief Cartwright asked.

"I need to go to the bathroom." Wayne's voice was adamant.

"I'm sorry, sir, but until everyone is cleared, and the CSIs have gathered the evidence, no one can wash their hands."

Wayne reached again for his zipper, and the chief, horrified, stepped back.

Enough was enough, thought Lilliana. It was time to get this situation under control before the assemblage of elderly residents with full bladders started an all out rebellion. She got up from her seat and headed over toward the door.

"Excuse me, Chief."

He turned hopeful eyes toward her. His expression pleaded with her to do something about the obstreperous old man confronting him.

"Surely it won't hurt to let us use the restrooms one at a time. As people get older, they don't have the, uh, capacity that they did when they were younger."

Several of the residents had come up behind her, obviously also in need of the restroom and anxious as to what the outcome of this discussion would be.

"But we might need to gather trace evidence, take fingerprints, and, uh…" He rubbed his jaw as he avoided her gaze.

"First of all, I don't think any of us committed the crime. Secondly, you can't just take fingerprints of everyone without their permission or a warrant. I don't believe you've had time to get a warrant for everyone in this room. And, lastly," she raised her hand and pointed a finger at him, "you—"

The chief's eyes riveted on her hand, still stained with blood.

"You're the one who discovered the body."

Lilliana glanced down at her finger and thought about Lady Macbeth obsessively washing her hands. *Is this a dagger I see before me?* Well, no, but it certainly looked just as incriminating.

"And our prime suspect," the chief added.

"Oh, tosh!" Lilliana exclaimed.

The chief's face set stone-like with determination. "For you, I have probable cause to collect evidence *and* fingerprints."

Lilliana sighed. Taking her prints didn't bother her. Every time she'd gotten a new librarian's job, one of the requirements was to be fingerprinted so they could assure she wasn't a criminal or a sex offender. There were probably several sets of prints for her in the system already. One more wouldn't make a difference. "How much longer until that happens? Wayne isn't the only one who needs to use the restroom you know."

Several heads nodded.

The chief, taking in the situation, deflated somewhat. "I suppose it wouldn't hurt to escort people to the restroom." He glanced over his shoulder and down the hallway, searching for someone for the job. "DeeDee," he called out. "Would you come here a minute?"

A moment later, a middle-aged woman with shoulder-length blonde hair appeared beside him. She smelled of apples and cinnamon, and Lilliana wondered if it was her perfume or if she'd been baking pies when she heard about the murder and, like so many others, come over to the retirement home out of curiosity.

"Afternoon, Chief. Got your hands full, don't you?" She looked up at the chief from under long, dark lashes.

Cartwright nodded. "Yes, I do. I could use some help here."

He turned his gaze toward the waiting group of seniors and said, "Would you please escort these folks, a few at a time, down to the restroom and make sure they come back?"

DeeDee's face clouded over. "I don't think toilet attendant is in the village secretary's job description."

"Please, DeeDee? Otherwise we might have a problem." He flicked a glance at Wayne, who smiled evilly, revealing coffee-stained dentures between his parted lips.

"Oh, all right. You—" she pointed at Wayne, then three others standing nearby "—and you, and you, and you. Come with me."

* * *

Lilliana took a seat at the table in the retirement community's library, a small room off the lobby of the main building. The crime techs had taken a sample of the blood on her hands— silly, because she'd told them where it came from—and allowed her to go to the ladies room and wash up. Now, if she could just have a cup of tea, she might feel civilized. The chief closed the door and took the chair opposite where she sat.

"I think the first thing you need to do is tell me how you found the body."

He really was young, thought Lilliana. How had a boy so inexperienced ever become chief of police? "Am I under arrest?" she asked with feigned innocence. She pressed her folded hands against her abdomen, trying to still the turmoil in her stomach.

Chief Cartwright raised his eyebrows and looked uncertain. "Why, no."

Lilliana gave a curt nod and said fiercely, "Good, because you haven't read me my Miranda rights."

He hesitated, and when he responded, his voice lacked authority. "I don't have to."

"That's right, but let me assure you that I know what they are. You can't make me stay here. Even if you think I'm a suspect. You *do* think I'm a suspect, don't you?"

"Everyone's a suspect," the chief said cautiously.

Lilliana was enjoying this little game of cat and mouse they were playing. In reality, she was just trying to find out how competent the young man was. If first impressions meant anything, he was in over his head.

She decided not to torture him further and launched into a detailed account of the afternoon, the missing button, and her search for a safety pin to hold her pants up. She still hadn't been able to accomplish that mission. They'd seized her equipment bag as evidence. She hoped they wouldn't keep it too long. There was softball practice on Wednesday, and she needed her glove, if not her bat, which she held little hope of getting back any time this century.

Cartwright made copious notes, apparently having trouble keeping up with her recitation as he scribbled rapidly. He was about to run out of paper in the notepad he'd taken from his shirt pocket.

"Several people mentioned you had an argument with the victim earlier today," Chief Cartwright said.

"That's right." It would have been silly to dispute that fact, since everyone in the room had heard her. "Of course, I wasn't the only one. Frank Bellandini told me that Bette had stolen his hybrid and was showing it as one she'd bred. He was quite irate."

"But wouldn't you characterize your disagreement as more…

uh… vocal than Mr. Bellandini's?"

"I'm not going to say any such thing." No sense adding fuel to the fire. It was obvious young Cartwright was looking for a quick solution to the crime. Lilliana could only imagine the pressure he was getting from Russ Ellison.

"Did anyone else go in the storage room today?"

"I'm sure I wouldn't know. I was at the show in the dining room all day. Oh, except when I took a break to have lunch on the patio. But after I put my equipment bag in the storage room, I had no reason to go back until I discovered the need for a safety pin."

The chief sat there for a few minutes, his face scrunched up as if trying to remember interrogation techniques from whatever police training he'd had before becoming Rainbow Ranch's lone law enforcement officer. He failed.

"I'll need a written statement from you," he said finally. "Please write—or type—one up and bring it to my office tomorrow."

Lilliana nodded, the chief's tone of voice indicating the end of the interview, arose from her chair, and left.

She stuck her head in the dining room, intending to find out if the show would go on as scheduled tomorrow, but no one was there. The other members of the African Violet Club had left their plants on the tables, so she decided that's what she would do as well. If there was no show tomorrow, she'd retrieve them then and bring them back to her apartment.

As long as she'd started in that direction, she determined to take a look around. Yellow crime scene tape crisscrossed the closed door to the storage room. She wondered how the staff would get access to the housekeeping supplies. They didn't do a full cleaning on Sunday, but someone ran a vacuum over the carpet in the public areas every day. It wasn't really her problem, but it might be if Shirley couldn't clean her apartment on Tuesday. Shirley only came every other week, and already the dust was accumulating. Not to mention the master bath. If there was one thing Lilliana insisted upon, it was a clean bathroom. Disinfected and sparkling. She wondered if the drug store in town carried cleaning supplies. She might have to clean the toilet herself if the crime scene wasn't released by Wednesday. Or Thursday at the latest.

She shook her head and looked at the closed door leading into the television room. Miguel no longer guarded it, so Lilliana opened the door and peeked in. It, too, was empty. Apparently she had been the last one to be questioned. *Saving the best for last?*

She wondered if they'd show the movie tonight. On the schedule was *My Fair Lady*, and she'd been looking forward to seeing it on a large screen with Surround Sound. And popcorn. She hardly ever ate popcorn, fearing damage to her dental work, but made an exception when she attended the weekly movie. Just a cup's worth, and she was very careful not to bite into any hard kernels. She'd have to stop at the reception desk and ask.

CHAPTER FIVE

Lilliana let herself into her apartment, shut the door behind her, and breathed a sigh of relief. She was glad to be home, surrounded by her plants. Four tiered, lighted plant stands, one on either side of the sofa and two in the far corner of the room, were lush with greenery and brightly colored flowers. The more experienced growers kept telling her she should focus on only one kind of cultivar, but so far she found that impossible to do. One four-tiered shelf unit held standards, another species plants, the third trailers, and the fourth miniatures. She loved them all.

The kitchen staff had left a covered tray on her dining room table. She wondered how long ago. She wasn't hungry, but she knew she should eat something. Lifting up the cover revealed a plate with institutionalized mystery meatloaf covered in a rubbery, congealed gravy that flowed over a lump of mashed potatoes. The vegetable du jour consisted of limp green beans with a few slivers of almonds. A dish of peaches served for dessert. No wonder she was never hungry.

She carried the tray into the kitchen and scraped the plates into the trash. After filling the kettle with water and setting it on the stove to boil, she headed toward the guest bathroom. She paused at the closed door on the opposite side of the hallway and placed her palm against it briefly before continuing to her destination.

She'd turned the guest bath into a plant nursery with shelves on the walls and planks across the tub to hold more pots. She checked the water level in the small humidifier that hummed on the floor. She raised her show plants here. The living room stayed on the dry side, despite a humidifier running day and night, which was why she'd gotten a second humidifier and set it up in the bathroom. Being smaller, the bathroom more easily kept the high humidity level the plants liked.

Now that she was here, she couldn't remember why she'd come. A "senior moment" was how most of the residents referred to this phenomenon. Lilliana couldn't help but worry those increasingly frequent moments were the first sign of dementia. She turned to leave, but before she could take a step into the hall, the reason came to her.

Since she'd sold most of the plants she'd taken to the show today, she went through the collection in the bathroom, mentally tagging those she'd bring down tomorrow. If there was a show tomorrow. She hadn't been able to get a definitive answer to that. The members of the club could see no reason the show shouldn't continue for the second day. The police chief didn't want his crime scene contaminated before he was ready to release it. Russ Ellison had disappeared sometime during the questioning sessions, but Lilliana's opinion was he'd just as soon not draw attention to the retirement home at this point in time.

The whistling of the tea kettle interrupted her musings.

A short time later, she carried a steaming mug of Earl Grey out to the patio and sat down with a sigh. Fortunate enough to live in a unit on the back side of the building near the end, the row of casitas at the rear of the complex didn't obstruct her view of the mountains. To the northeast the sky was already darkening to black velvet. The evening star, Venus this time of year if she remembered correctly from the newspaper, shone bright low in the sky.

She settled back in her chair. Her favorite time was when the quiet night wrapped her in a cloak of darkness, and she could congratulate herself on making it through another day. And what a day it had been. Poor Bette. As much as she didn't like the woman, she had had no desire to see her killed. *Who could possibly have disliked her so much they'd resorted to murder?*

Lilliana felt somewhat chagrined that she'd supplied the murder weapon. If she hadn't left her softball bat in the storage room, would Bette still be alive? She shook off that idea. It wasn't her fault Bette had been murdered. Although that young chief of police seemed to think it was—and not just as supplier of the murder weapon.

How in the world had he gotten the job? He'd appeared as lost as a weekend hiker plunked down in the Catalina Mountains without a compass. She hoped he'd be getting some help from the Cochise County Sheriff's Office. She had no idea how these things worked, particularly in Rainbow Ranch. She'd grown up in Boston, spent many years in Tucson, both of which had a proper police department with a major crimes division staffed by multiple detectives.

She touched her lips to the liquid in her cup to test the temperature, then, finding it cool enough to drink, took a long sip. *Ahhhh.* There was something comforting about a good cup of tea.

A coyote pack yipped and howled in the distance, sending a shiver up Lilliana's spine. Wildlife in Arizona didn't respect city limits. Even in Tucson coyotes strolled along washes near major roadways, trotted down sidewalks in residential areas in the early morning. The retirement community even had its own resident bobcat. The first time Lilliana saw him, she'd been concerned and reported it to the receptionist. The woman laughed and told her about the cat's privileged status. Bobcats were relatively small. Lilliana hoped the receptionist would show a little more concern if she reported a mountain lion.

Her skin tingled with the sensation of a light breeze, chilling her even though the air was still. The red flower tufts on the bush separating her patio from her neighbor's seemed to flutter at the edge of her vision. The hour was too late for the hummingbirds that usually fed on the nectar of the Baja fairy duster. She turned her head and caught a tiny fading shower of sparkles, as if someone had tossed a thimbleful of glitter in the air. *It must be a trick of the light.*

As she examined the foliage edging her patio, there was nothing there. Whatever it was had disappeared. If it had been there to begin with. *First forgetting things, now seeing things. Is this what she had to look forward to?*

The night air was cooling and, along with it, her tea. With almost no humidity, the desert air quickly lost its heat once the sun left the sky. She should go inside anyway and type up that statement for the chief. She wanted to bring it to him in the morning and get everything settled as quickly as possible.

She opened the sliding glass door and stepped into the darkened living room. The automatic timer had turned off the plant lights, leaving the room in inky blackness. Lilliana flipped on a lamp, banishing the shadows.

After rinsing out her mug, she retrieved her laptop from the bedroom and sat on the sofa to type her statement. An hour later, she re-read it with a frown on her lips and a crease between her eyebrows. She'd taken so long because she wanted to be sure she not only had the facts right, but that they didn't implicate her in the killing. On a second read, she wondered if she hadn't made a case for *the lady doth protest too much*.

CHAPTER SIX

Lilliana shuffled down the aisle of Canyon Road Presbyterian Church on her way out, hemmed in by people in front and behind. When the club had first planned the show she'd wondered if she might have to skip services this morning, but everyone agreed they should schedule a later opening—eleven o'clock—on Sunday, so there was plenty of time to attend church at nine o'clock.

Several people nodded and smiled at her, and she returned the nods and smiles with her own. She didn't know anyone, other than by sight, except the minister, Pastor Douglas, of course, whom she'd spoken to briefly when she'd first started attending. The congregation consisted mostly of town people. Few, if any, of the residents of the retirement community ever went, except on holidays like Christmas and Easter.

That was another thing Russell Ellison had overlooked when converting the old ranch to a retirement home. Few of the residents were Presbyterian, and as that was the denomination of the only church in town, few attended. Once a month they ran a minivan into Benson and made a circuit of the churches there, with a stop for brunch at a restaurant, but for the other three, or sometimes four, Sundays, most just didn't attend.

Lilliana had been one of the non-attenders until recently herself. She hadn't been too pleased with God and what he'd done in her life. But about a month ago, as she drank her evening tea on her patio, she'd watched the stars come out one by one until they covered the sky. It had been a moonless night, so she'd been able to pick out the nebula in Orion, if she didn't look at it head-on. She'd started thinking about the vastness of the universe and the number of stars and planets and galaxies that filled it and how Someone must have created it.

And there was the fact of her own mortality. While generally healthy and active, she was in what was certainly the last quarter of her life, if not the last decade. As Shakespeare had said in Hamlet:

Thou know'st 'tis common; all that lives must die,
Passing through nature to eternity.

And so she decided it was time to come to an accommodation, if not a relationship, with God.

"Good morning, Lilliana," the minister greeted her when she finally reached the door. "Will you be joining us for coffee this morning?"

Pastor Douglas had asked her that question every week since she'd started coming. Unsure about how involved in this church she wanted to be, she'd avoided socializing with the members. She knew from experience that if she started to participate in the life of the church, she'd be persuaded to do more and more, until her time was hardly her own. But she'd started running out of excuses. Fortunately, this week she had a totally valid one. "Sorry, Pastor Douglas. I have to get back in time for the African violet show. Maybe next week."

"I'll be looking forward to seeing you then."

Lilliana mumbled something unintelligible and hurried out.

It was a quick walk down Canyon Road, with a left turn on Main Street, and then up the drive to the retirement home. The drive was lined with cars, many of them with out-of-state license plates. Cars filled the parking lot as well, and a crowd milled around in front of the entrance, grumbling to themselves and one another.

What in the world was going on?

It didn't take long for Lilliana to figure it out. As she passed through the crowd, she overheard what most people were talking about.

"Do you think we'll be able to see where they found the body?"

"I hear that old woman was pretty angry."

Lilliana couldn't help but think that one referred to her, despite the fact that "old woman" wasn't a very distinguishing characteristic given the setting.

"Someone said this wasn't the first resident who died here."

Lilliana rolled her eyes and pushed her way through the crowd. "Excuse me, can I get through?"

A middle-aged man turned his angry glare on her. "Get to the end of the line, lady. Wait your turn. We've been waiting thirty minutes to get in."

"Maybe so, young man, but I live here."

Heads swiveled in her direction, and the crowd hushed at her announcement. The man's anger turned to confusion as he puzzled out whether that allowed her to move to the head of the line or not. The woman next to him—his wife?—touched Lilliana lightly on the arm. "Did you see her? Did you see the body? What was it like?"

Opting not to answer the question, Lilliana elbowed her way to the glass doors and grasped the handle of one. Unsurprisingly in light of the crowd, the door was locked. She rapped on the glass to get the attention of the worried woman behind the reception desk. When the receptionist recognized Lilliana, she picked up a key ring and came toward the door. She turned the key in the lock and opened the door a crack.

"Let me in, Beverly," Lilliana said.

Beverly's eyes flicked to the people standing behind her. "I'm afraid all these people will come rushing in if I do that, Mrs. Wentworth. Mr. Ellison has already gone to fetch the chief. Maybe it would be best if you stayed out there until he gets back."

"Don't be silly. These people aren't storming the Bastille. I'm sure they'll wait patiently until we open for the African violet show. Let me come in now." Lilliana turned around and gave the waiting crowd her best reference librarian stern look. Apparently most of them had been to a library, because the tide of humanity ebbed just a bit.

"Well, okay," Beverly said, still apprehensive, but she opened the door wide enough for Lilliana to enter. As soon as she was inside, Beverly closed the door and firmly locked it again, sighing with relief as she did so. When she lowered her hands, Lilliana noticed they were shaking.

"I'm sure everything will be all right," Lilliana said, although she was a bit surprised at the turnout of ghouls looking for a chance to observe an actual crime scene. Most of them must have come from outside of Rainbow Ranch, Benson maybe, or even Tucson, although Tucson certainly had its share of murders, and there really was no reason for Tucsonans to come all the way to Rainbow Ranch to see one.

"Are we going to have the show today?" Lilliana asked. She was still hoping to sell more plants and leaves. Not that it would put a dent in her electric bill. Those lights and humidifiers running ten hours a day resulted in alarming statements from the electric company. Now that the show was over, she'd see what she could do about cutting back on those hours, particularly of the lights, without causing too much damage to her plants.

"I don't know. I didn't get a chance to ask Mr. Ellison, but I hope not."

Lilliana bit her lip. Being optimistic, she said, "Well, I'm going to fill in my plant display just in case, and make sure everyone's ready for the opening."

The quiet in her apartment was a relief after the tumult outside. She wasn't sure which way Russ Ellison would lean. Would he cancel the show, fearing more bad publicity, or, like actors were quoted as saying, feel that there was no such thing as bad publicity and let them in, hoping to salvage his promotion of the retirement community? She hoped the latter. Then another thought came to her. Would the young chief of police have anything to say about it?

She gathered up the plants she'd selected last night, placed them on the kitchen counter for staging, and stood for a minute trying to figure out how to carry them down to the dining room. The cart she'd used yesterday was still behind the crime scene tape. A cardboard box would work, but she didn't have any, having long ago thrown out the boxes she'd used to move in two years ago.

Ah! It came to her in a flash of brilliance. Or what passed for brilliance in her nowadays. Bending down, she opened the large drawer under the oven and pulled out the turkey roaster. She should easily be able to fit six plants in it. Once she'd loaded the plants and bagged leaves in the pan, she headed for the dining room.

As she passed through the lobby, she saw Chief Cartwright, pointedly wearing a dress blue uniform, standing outside the door with Russ Ellison and Dale Ackerman, the mayor of Rainbow Ranch. She was somewhat surprised to see the mayor, but he probably thought he had a dog in this hunt, seeing as it was an election year. He wouldn't want to miss an opportunity to be seen acting mayorly. The three of them had their heads bent together, either to be able to hear one another or to keep what they were discussing from the crowd. Lilliana paused, then walked toward the door to try to hear what they were saying.

Mayor Ackerman raised his head and looked over the crowd. "Now, folks, I know you've all traveled a ways to see the African violet show, and we don't want to disappoint you. But there are quite a few more people than will fit inside comfortably. Since we want to make sure you all get a good view of the flowers, we're going to let you in a few at a time. As people come out again, we'll let more people in."

It sounded like a reasonable plan to Lilliana. She turned and continued to the dining room. Most of the club members were inside and working on their displays, grooming plants, adding bagged leaves, rearranging things to present the most pleasing positioning in hopes of encouraging a sale. Like herself, almost all the retirees could use the extra money. They looked up as she entered, questions on their faces.

Lilliana walked to her table and put the turkey roaster full of plants down, then turned to face the group and nodded. "We're a go for today. I just heard the mayor announce they'd be letting people in a few at a time."

A collective sigh went up. It appeared the desire to sell and show off plants was stronger than their respect for the now-departed Bette Tesselink. The club members returned to what they'd been doing before Lilliana entered the room.

As she started moving the hybrids already on her table to make room for the new arrivals, Lenny spoke up. "Good job, Lilliana."

She stopped putting out the new additions and looked at him, wondering what "good job" he was talking about. Then it dawned on her. "Oh, I had nothing to do with it. All I did was hear what the mayor said after discussing it with Ellison and that young policeman."

"You're too modest. I'm sure you had some influence in the decision."

Lilliana was going to protest again, but decided it was useless. When Lenny made up his mind, there was little anyone could do to convince him otherwise.

The sound of footsteps hurriedly tapping on the tile floor erupted outside the dining room. They must have let the first group in. Lilliana crossed her fingers and hoped they were in a buying mood. A dozen or so people came through the entrance and looked around as if they thought they might see a body at any moment. Most of them descended on poor Mary, since her table was closest to the door.

"Where did they find the dead woman?"

"Do you know who killed her?"

A barrage of questions assaulted the shy, diminutive Mary, who was clearly overwhelmed by the attention. Lilliana hurried to her rescue.

"I'm sure you'll understand that we have been asked by the police not to discuss the distressing events of yesterday with anyone." Lilliana wondered where that came from. Probably from reading too many mysteries and watching endless reruns of *Law and Order*. The chief had said no such thing, although he should have. Another example of his inexperience. "There's still an active investigation at this time. Meanwhile, we have lots of lovely plants to show you. And sell to you, if you'd like to own one."

Disappointment flooded the faces of the attendees. At least half of them headed for the door, but the other half decided to make the best of it and spread out among the display tables.

"Are you all right, Mary?" Lilliana asked.

Mary smiled weakly. "Yes, thank you. And thank you for coming over here and rescuing me. They were all so pushy, and I had no idea what to say to them."

Lilliana patted her on the shoulder. "It was no trouble. I just hope every group doesn't start out like the first one."

Alarm filled Mary's eyes at the thought of having to go through that again, and Lilliana regretted saying what she had. But it was better for Mary to be prepared. At least, she thought so.

"I'm sure everything will be all right now. When they go out, they'll probably tell everyone we're not talking."

Reassured, Mary tried to erase the concern from her face, but wasn't entirely successful.

"I'll come back if you need me," Lilliana added.

"Thank you, Lilliana."

"Good job, Lily," Lenny said again when she got back behind her table. "You always get to the heart of things and fix them."

"I'm not so sure I can fix this," Lilliana confided. "I'm afraid most of the people who came today are much more interested in the murder than in our African violets."

Proving her point, a trio of women in their late fifties approached her table. They pretended to look at the plants for a few seconds, then the middle one, a woman with red hair of a shade which certainly came out of a bottle, turned her attention to Lilliana. "You seem to know what's going on here," she began. "Did you see the dead woman? Do you know what happened?"

The person on her right, a short, chubby woman with tightly-permed, steel-gray curls and eyes as big as saucers, poked the redhead in the ribs with an elbow. "Don't you recognize her from the news? She's the one who found the body!"

"Is that right?" the other woman asked.

Before Lilliana could respond, a light so bright it would have blinded her had she been looking at it exploded in front of her. To her dismay, a television crew stood behind the trio of women. They must have been let in when the looky-lous from the first group left.

Biff Buckley, having wedged himself between the tables to

stand beside her, stuck a microphone in front of her face. "Aren't you afraid to live here now that there's been a murder?"

Refusing to give the obnoxious reporter fuel for the media storm he was trying to stir up, Lilliana replied firmly, "Certainly not. Unless *you're* thinking of murdering me?"

"We'll cut that," he said in an aside to the cameraman, then, resuming his role as star television reporter, asked, "What did you feel when you heard Bette Tesselink had been murdered?"

"Feel?" Lilliana thought about it for a moment. "Well, I was horrified, of course. You don't expect to find someone you know murdered like that."

"Are you saying you found the body?" Biff's voice was filled with a false eagerness as if he'd just discovered this potential scoop. Ludicrous, of course, since he'd come directly to her when he entered the room.

Now Lilliana felt chagrined. She hadn't meant to confirm her involvement in the crime. But it was too late now. She'd already given herself away. "I did."

"How was she murdered?" The reporter's excitement was palpable. He was having a hard time to keep from jumping up and down.

If the reporter didn't know already, Lilliana didn't think it was her place to tell him. She fell back on the statements she'd made outside the door before he arrived.

"But surely our viewers have a right to know," Biff prodded.

"I think Chief Cartwright would disagree with that." Although, it might be kind of fun to describe the blood and the bat with just a little exaggeration, if only to see the reporter wet his pants from excitement. *Now, now. Act your age.* A smile crept to her lips. Actually, that was her age. One of the benefits of being elderly was you were allowed to not care what other people thought. You could get away with an awful lot once you retired. People almost expected some outrageous behavior.

"Can you tell me what you're thinking now?"

Oops! Obviously Buckley had noticed the smile. Lilliana got herself under control and said in measured tones, "I'm thinking I've said all I'm going to say. Please leave my table so these people can have a look at my African violets."

The reporter, realizing he'd gotten about as much out of Lilliana as he was going to, lowered the microphone and said to the cameraman, "Cut it, Joe."

Thankfully, the cameraman doused the spotlight, and the two of them moved off in search of better candidates for their news coverage. Once the spots in front of her eyes cleared, she saw she had gathered quite a large crowd. Or, rather, the TV crew had. Now that they'd moved on, the group started to disperse. Except for the original trio of fifty-somethings and a few others.

The redhead pointed at the True Blue hybrid and asked, "How much is that one?"

Lilliana hadn't intended on selling her prize plant, but, on second thought, she had several more growing in her guest bath, none quite as well-developed as this one, but certainly plants that could be groomed up to show quality within a relatively short time. "Twenty-five dollars."

The woman's friend was outraged. "Oh, Doris. That's much too expensive for a houseplant."

Doris looked at her disdainfully. "This isn't an ordinary houseplant. It was grown by the woman who discovered the body. Maybe by the murderer herself."

All eyes turned back to Lilliana. A wave of dizziness passed over her. She thought about protesting, but the redhead was already digging in her purse. She opened her wallet and took out a twenty dollar bill, added a five, and handed the money over to Lilliana. The dizziness passed, and she shook off the shock.

"Here you are, madam," Lilliana said, picking up the plant and handing it to Doris, who took it with a triumphant look. "I hope you enjoy it."

"Oh, I'm sure I will." The three women hurried away, chatting excitedly among themselves.

Lilliana watched them go, then was called back by the gravelly voice of a middle-aged woman asking, "Do you have another one of those?"

Those who had not deserted her table when the television crew left surged forward, each one of them eager to buy a souvenir from the suspected murderess.

CHAPTER SEVEN

Lilliana entered the dining room—which was once again a dining room and not an event hall—and sat down. White, crisp linen covered the round tables returned from the patio, and the flatware at each place gleamed bright and shiny. She picked up the day's menu from where it lay on the floral-patterned china plate and deliberated between the oatmeal with fresh fruit and scrambled eggs with bacon and toast. Since she had errands to run in town and might decide to stop at the restaurant—there was only one restaurant in Rainbow Ranch—she opted for oatmeal. She could always use the fiber.

Right after she placed her order, Frank came into the dining room with Nancy Gardner. Frank spied her and headed toward her table.

"Mind if we join you?" he asked.

Lilliana shook her head. "Not at all. In fact, I was hoping to talk to you this morning."

"Oh?" Frank took the seat to her right, while Nancy sat in the next one over.

"Good morning," Nancy said. "Did you get a chance to try my peach pie yesterday?"

As promised, Nancy had shown up with the peach pie with chili powder to share with those eating on the patio yesterday afternoon. Lilliana, who was just finishing lunch with Mary, made a hasty exit, thereby avoiding either tasting something that sounded positively nasty, or hurting Nancy's feelings by refusing a piece of the pie. "No, unfortunately, I didn't."

"I have some left over," Nancy said eagerly. "I could bring a piece to your apartment after breakfast."

"That would be lovely," Lilliana replied, "only I'm going out as soon as I finish eating." She didn't mention she intended to make a stop back at her apartment to pick up the statement for Chief Cartwright.

"A secret liaison?" Frank teased.

"I can only hope." Lilliana laughed. "No, actually I need to bring my statement to the police department. Did you have to write one, Frank?"

Frank nodded. "Yes. I gave it to that young officer Saturday when he was here."

"Oh." Lilliana was somewhat disappointed. She'd been hoping Frank would take the walk into town with her. Just for company. "In that case, do you know where the police department is? I've never seen it on my walks into town."

It was Frank's turn to laugh. "It's in City Hall. Everything's in City Hall—the mayor's office, the fire department, the police department. You know where that is, right?"

"Oh, of course." City Hall was at the opposite end of Rainbow Ranch from the church, near the elementary school, whose baseball field Lilliana and her team used for softball practice every Wednesday. An easy walk from the retirement community. Then again, everything in Rainbow Ranch was an easy walk from the retirement community.

"Any news on the murder?" Frank paused to order scrambled eggs when the waitress came back with Lilliana's hot water. "I see they've taken down the crime scene tape."

Nancy ordered pastries and coffee, then asked if they had Tabasco sauce. The woman must have no taste buds.

"I hadn't noticed that. That's good news. I was afraid I'd miss my apartment cleaning this week." She stopped to ponder his question about the murder. It seemed her brain was processing the conversation in reverse this morning and had finally gotten to what Frank said first. At least she remembered everything. She congratulated herself for that. Then doubt slipped in. Would she know she'd forgotten something if she didn't remember it?

Frank was staring at her. "The murder?" he said.

Lilliana hastened to reply. "Why would you think I'd know anything new about the murder?" She probably shouldn't have been surprised, since she was suspect number one, but she was.

"Oh, you know…" Frank's voice trailed off and the tops of his ears turned red.

"I'll see what I can find out today," Lilliana said and realized she meant it. She was curious as to what Chief Cartwright had discovered so far, and what his plans were to proceed with the investigation.

"Such a terrible thing," Nancy said.

The waitress showed up with more coffee for Frank and Nancy. "Your oatmeal will be out in a minute," she said to Lilliana and headed off again.

"Who would kill Bette Tesselink?" Nancy asked.

That was the question of the hour, of course. Although Lilliana couldn't think of a single person who liked the woman, no one disliked her enough to kill her. At least, not to her knowledge. "Well, there must be one person. All we have to do is find out who it is."

"We?" Frank asked.

"Well, the police." The slip of the tongue disconcerted her. She hadn't intended to say "we," but the word had popped out all the same.

Apparently Frank had the same reservations she did. "If I thought we could help that young man, I'd certainly volunteer."

"Well, I'm sure he'll manage to handle it," Lilliana said with more confidence than she felt.

"You're probably right."

The food arrived, and the three of them set to eating it, none of them wanting to explore further how the murder would be solved.

* * *

It felt good to stretch her legs after two whole days spent inside at the African Violet Club Show. She walked around the circle of grass with the gazebo at its center, admiring the way the white wood stood out against the cerulean blue sky. She sometimes brought a book out to the gazebo to read, especially during the week when there wouldn't be a lot of vehicle traffic to disturb her.

She shifted the bag she carried over her shoulder. The strap cut into her flesh from the weight of the potted plant inside. Mr. Pulaski had never come back for his purchase, probably because of all the to-do over the murder, and she intended to drop the African violet off after her visit to Chief Cartwright and before lunch at Cathy's Café. She could make a circle, down Pulaski Street to City Hall, then down School Street to the intersection at Canyon Road, where the church was, and up Canyon Road to Main Street, on the corner of which was Pulaski's Gourmet Grocery. Then down Main to the café, and, afterwards, a leisurely walk back to the retirement community.

She stopped at the traffic light on Main Street which needlessly glared red in her direction. There was no traffic to stop at this time of the morning. The "rush hour," which probably took about ten minutes sometime around seven-thirty, was long over. But Lilliana obeyed the law, so she stood watching the empty roadway in front of her until the light turned green.

The walk down Pulaski Street went quickly since it was, literally, down. Rainbow Ranch sat in a valley and sloped gently up toward the mountains northeast of the retirement community. You couldn't miss City Hall. It sat at the end of Pulaski Street, a red brick building dating from sometime in the 1800s. There must be a clay deposit close by, thought Lilliana, for it to be made of red bricks. Most construction in Arizona, especially in the early days, was done with brown adobe. Lumber was too expensive to ship from the mountain country to the north, and steel would have to come in from the east via rail, so it was cheaper to use the materials at hand and make adobe. She wondered why she'd never noticed the red brick before.

Lilliana climbed the steps, opened the door, and looked left and right. She hadn't expected to see anything to the right, the large garage doors to the fire department having been obvious from the outside. Although a counter took up most of the center of the lobby, no one stood behind it to ask questions of. Straight ahead, a pair of large frosted glass doors labeled Council Room loomed. In the far left corner, gold letters spelling out Mayor's Office were etched on another imposing door. Turning her head, she saw a modest door labeled Rainbow Ranch Police Department. Not terribly impressive, but for a one-person department, she supposed it didn't have to be.

She knocked, then opened the door a crack to peek inside.

The weary face of the young police officer met her gaze. "Oh, it's you."

"May I come in?" Lilliana asked.

He waved a hand toward the chair in front of his desk. "Certainly."

It only took a couple of steps for Lilliana to cross from the door to the chair. The office couldn't have been more than ten feet long by ten feet wide. Most of the space was taken up by the chief's desk, chair, and a couple of filing cabinets on the wall to her right. A window on her left filtered dim light through a layer of dust. Seeing the state of the office, she checked the chair before sitting on it.

"What can I do for you?" The chief's eyes were red from staring at the computer screen in front of him, and his shoulders drooped.

Lilliana opened her purse, pulled out the statement she'd printed from her computer, unfolded it, and laid it on the chief's desk, smoothing out the creases before folding her hands in her lap. "I brought the statement you asked for."

"Thank you." Chief Cartwright picked up the sheet of paper

and scanned through the statement. When he finished, he looked up, met her eyes with his own, and said, "This seems to be exactly what you told me the day of the murder."

Lilliana nodded. "It is, to the best of my ability. May I go now?"

Before the chief could answer, the mayor stuck his head in the door. He looked harried as he asked, "Any progress on the case yet, Chad?"

"Not so far, Uncle Dale. I'm waiting for the ME's report to see if there are any leads there. The CSI unit called me and said there were a ton of fingerprints in the storage room, and it would take a few weeks for them to process them all."

"See if you can light a fire under those folks. The media is eating me alive on this." With that, the mayor closed the door, leaving Lilliana alone with the overwrought police chief.

The chief seemed to have forgotten she was sitting there. Maybe that had something to do with the fact that the mayor had treated her as if she were invisible.

"May I go now?" Lilliana repeated.

"Oh, I'm sorry," Chief Cartwright said. "Is there anything else you can remember? Anything at all?" Although he kept his voice level, his face pleaded with her to come up with something. "Anything about your relationship with the deceased?"

"We barely had a relationship." Did the chief really think she was the murderer? "I'm sorry, young man. Everything I know is in my statement."

"Well, if you do think of anything else, please call me right away." The chief took a business card from the holder on his desk and held it out to her. "You can go."

After accepting the card and glancing at it, Lilliana put it in her purse and rose from the chair. "Good day," she said, then added in a more sympathetic tone of voice, "I hope the crime scene people come up with something for you."

"Me, too." He looked younger than ever.

Well, that's one mystery solved, she thought as she strode down School Street. Obviously, the reason Chad Cartwright had gotten the job of chief of police was because his uncle was mayor of Rainbow Ranch. It didn't surprise her. Although technically a civil service position, how many ambitious policemen would be interested in a job in a sleepy town like this one?

A class on the school playground was enjoying the fine weather. The softball field sat empty, and that reminded Lilliana she had forgotten to ask about her equipment bag. With practice on Wednesday, she would like her ball and glove back. She'd have to give the chief a call later.

She swung onto Canyon Road and picked up her pace even though the street sloped uphill. She was eager to drop off Mr. Pulaski's African violet and get to the restaurant for lunch. The thought crossed her mind that maybe the idea of lunch wasn't the only thing prompting her to hurry, but she quickly pushed it aside.

Ted Pulaski looked up from a pile of papers on the counter when the bell over the door rang. "Mrs. Wentworth," he greeted her. "So good to see you."

He appeared genuinely glad to see her; a broad smile covered his face and reminded her of the expression grinning from ear to ear. Lillian returned the smile. "Good to see you as well, Mr. Pulaski."

"Ted. Call me Ted. Everyone does."

"And you should call me Lilliana." Funny, in all the months she'd been coming into his store, they'd never gone through the ceremony of using their first names before.

"I got in another shipment of Earl Grey tea," Ted offered. "And some of that dark chocolate you like." His eyes went to the display of candy in front of the counter.

"How nice," Lilliana said. "But I didn't come here to buy anything."

"Oh?"

"Did you forget your African violet? When you didn't come in to pick it up, I thought I'd best bring it to you." Lilliana carefully put the tote bag on the counter and extracted the plant. She flicked at the leaves with a finger, then turned it to make sure the violet had survived the trip intact.

"I didn't think you'd have the show yesterday." Ted looked surprised. "What with the murder and all."

"Fortunately, everyone agreed that the show must go on," Lilliana said. She'd thought that might have been the reason Mr. Pulaski—Ted—hadn't shown up yesterday. At least, she'd hoped that was the reason, and not that he'd changed his mind about the plant.

"Well, then, I'm sorry I didn't come by and caused you the trouble of making the trip." He rubbed his face as if trying to scrub away the regret that had come over it. "Let me give you one of those chocolate bars you like so much. We'll call it a delivery fee." He took one from the display and held it out to her.

Flustered, Lilliana said, "Oh, it wasn't any trouble. I had to come into town and drop my statement off at the police department anyway." She regarded the proffered chocolate, hesitant to accept the gift.

"Please take it," Ted urged.

She considered for a moment longer, then took the chocolate and put it in her purse. It would go very well with her evening cup of Earl Grey.

"Thank you. I feel much better about not coming to pick up the plant," Ted said. "And now I suppose you'll be heading off to see our fine police chief."

"Oh, oh no," Lilliana said. "I've already been. I'm going to eat lunch at the café now. A little treat for myself." She smiled as if to let him know this was a rare indulgence. Which it was. There wasn't a whole lot left of her pension check after she'd paid the retirement community for her apartment and meals.

Ted brightened. "I don't suppose you'd like some company?"

If she had been flustered before, she was now completely rattled. Was he asking to go to lunch with her? Calm down, Lilliana, she told herself. You're behaving like a schoolgirl. Why shouldn't you have lunch with Mr. Pulaski? It wasn't as if he was asking her for a date. "Why, that would be very nice. But don't you have to mind the store?"

"I always close at noon for lunch. I'm not too busy on most days. Just let me grab my jacket from the back."

Lilliana nodded, not sure she could trust her voice, and watched as he hurried down the aisle to the back of the store. For a ninety-year old, he moved nimbly. And he didn't look too bad, either. He hadn't gone to fat, like so many men did. In fact, he was a little on the thin side. Not that she should talk. In her younger days, she would have described her current figure as skinny.

Wearing a corduroy jacket, Ted emerged from the back and jogged to the front of the store. "Ready?" he asked and held out his arm.

Lilliana took his arm, and together they headed out. Ted paused at the door to switch the sign from Open to Will Be Back At and pushed the hands the cardboard clock until they registered 1:00 P.M. After closing and locking the door, he extended his arm to Lilliana once more and they proceeded down Main Street.

Lilliana was glad the street was empty. She didn't want to be seen going to lunch with Ted Pulaski. Not that she was embarrassed about it. Well, maybe a little. Her real fear was the teasing she'd get if any of the retirement home residents saw them together. Comfortable in their second childhood, many of the people she knew would gleefully tease her about having a boyfriend, just like in grade school. She was having enough trouble holding onto her dignity as it was.

"Lovely day, isn't it?" she said to fill the silence around them.

"Yes, it is," Ted agreed. "And a lovely lady to spend it with."

Lilliana felt herself blushing. The situation was getting out of control. Fortunately, it didn't take them too long to walk to the intersection of Main and Pulaski, where Cathy's Café was situated. For the first time, Lilliana noticed the name of the street. "Why, this is Pulaski Street."

"Yes, it is." Ted was grinning. When she didn't respond, he added, "It used to be called Pulaski Way on the other side of Main Street, too, before I sold the ranch to Russell Ellison."

"You mean you used to own that land?" Lilliana was trying to adjust to the idea of the man beside her having been the owner of such a huge property. The man whom she had thought of as the modest town grocer was probably very rich.

"Yes, I did." Ted opened the door to the restaurant and held it while Lilliana entered. "I'll tell you about it after we get a table."

Cathy sat them at a table near the front window. They could see traffic going by and the road that used to be Pulaski Way leading into the retirement community across the street. Lilliana picked up the menu and pretended to examine its contents while she got used to the idea of Ted Pulaski not being just this pleasant elderly man who owned a grocery store. When she peeked out from behind the menu, Ted hadn't picked his up. He was looking at her instead.

Quickly, she looked back at her choices and decided on a tuna salad sandwich. She put the menu down and folded her hands. "Aren't you going to look at the menu?" she asked.

"Don't have to," Ted said. "I come here just about every day, if not for lunch, then for dinner. I know the menu by heart. The specials, too. Would you like to know what today's specials are?"

"It's not necessary. I know what I want."

"In that case, let's order." A waitress leaned against the counter, chatting with a customer. When she saw Ted wave, she hurried over.

"What can I get you today, Mr. Pulaski?" the waitress asked.

"Ladies first. Lilliana?"

"I'll have the tuna salad sandwich. On whole wheat, if you have it," Lilliana said. "And tea. Iced tea."

The waitress turned to Ted, pad and pencil ready.

"I'll have the meat loaf special," Ted said.

"Thank you." The waitress gathered up the menus and

headed for the kitchen.

Ted took a sip from his water glass.

"Tell me about the ranch," Lilliana said.

"It's a long story," Ted said.

"That's fine with me. I don't have anything else to do today." Then, realizing he did, she added, "Why don't you give me the Reader's Digest version?"

"Do they still publish that?" Ted asked.

"I think so," Lilliana said. "I seem to remember seeing a copy in my dentist's office the last time I went."

"I remember my mother had a whole shelf full of those condensed books," Ted said. "She couldn't wait for a new one to arrive." He stared off into the distance for a moment. "But you wanted to hear about the ranch."

Lilliana nodded.

"My grandfather came out to Arizona in the eighteen-seventies," Ted began. "After the Civil War, the South was pretty tore up. He wanted a new start for his family, something to wipe away all the bad memories."

"What made him choose Arizona?" Lilliana asked.

"I thought you wanted the Reader's Digest version?" Ted's eyes twinkled.

"Oh, I'm sorry. Go ahead and tell it your way. I'll try to save my questions for another time."

"Don't trouble yourself about that," Ted said. He lifted his hand as if he were about to place it on hers, then put it back down on the table. "He was out here during the war. He took part in the Battle of Picacho Peak. It wasn't much of a battle, but it got him out here, and he liked the desert climate and the mountains. His idea was to raise cattle and be free of the cities."

Ted paused for another drink of water. The waitress came back with their luncheons. Not only was the sandwich huge, it came with a pile of potato chips and a pickle on the side. Looking at Ted's plate, Lilliana was glad she hadn't ordered the meatloaf. There were three slices, a hill of mashed potatoes, and a serving of peas and carrots that would have made a meal in itself. Lilliana picked up a half sandwich and took a delicate bite. Ted broke off a chunk of meatloaf and put it in his mouth. While he chewed, Lilliana took a packet of sugar from the container on the table, tore it open, and stirred it into her tea.

Ted swallowed the meatloaf. "This is going to take longer than I thought if I'm going to eat at the same time. Anyway, my grandfather, Stan—short for Stanislaw—Pulaski, once he made sure his wife and children would be okay on their own for a few months, came back to Arizona to look for ranch land. He got off the train in Tucson and asked around for where he should go. Folks advised him to stay away from Tombstone, which was a pretty rough town in those days. Somehow he heard about the land out here."

Another pause for meatloaf, this time with a topping of mashed potatoes and gravy. Lilliana had eaten most of the first half of her sandwich. She picked up a potato chip and popped it in her mouth. Surely it wouldn't hurt to have just one.

The waitress, carrying a pitcher of ice water, stopped at their table. "How is everything?" she asked as she refilled Ted's glass.

Since Ted was chewing, Lilliana replied. "Everything is very good."

"Anything else I can get you folks?"

Ted answered that one. "I think we're all set."

The waitress went back to the counter and her conversation with the other customer.

Ted continued his story. "Stan rode out on horseback to check the place out. It was monsoon season, and he ran into some pretty rough weather, but as soon as he hit the spot where that gazebo is now, the sun broke through the clouds, and a rainbow arced across the sky. He figured the rainbow was a sign. Bought the place as soon as he got back to Tucson and sent for Grandma Wanda and the kids. By the time they arrived, he'd built a little house near the creek up there."

"Creek?" Lilliana couldn't remember seeing a creek.

"Well, it's kind of a trickle now. It used to run a lot stronger back then," Ted said with a smile. "But it's fresh water. If you walk into the hills behind the casitas, you'll run into a little pond if there's been rain. Kind of a mud flat if there hasn't."

Lilliana was thinking she'd have to take a hike up that way. Like most desert rats, she was drawn to open water like a kitten to a toy with feathers. Even if the creek was just a trickle, it would be pretty to look at.

Lilliana had finished the first half of her sandwich and, to her amazement, most of the pile of potato chips. So much for "just one." She waved at the waitress.

"Can I have a to-go box?" Lilliana asked once the waitress reached their table.

Ted, who had taken the opportunity of the pause in their conversation to consume more of his lunch, raised his eyebrows. "Is that all you're gonna eat?"

"It's a big sandwich," Lilliana said. "Half is more than enough for me. I'll have the rest for lunch tomorrow."

The waitress returned quickly with the Styrofoam container, and Lilliana, before she could change her mind, put the remaining half of her sandwich inside and closed the lid. "So," she said, hoping to get Ted's mind off her lack of appetite and back on the history of the ranch, "did your grandfather raise cattle?"

"He sure did. Ran a pretty good herd on the open range here. My father helped out almost as soon as he could walk. Sisters, too. When grandpa passed, my dad took over running the ranch. Sent me off to school at the U of A, hoping I'd find something I liked to do that paid better than ranching. It didn't work." Ted grinned. "Guess ranching was in my bones."

"How did you become a shopkeeper?" Lilliana asked.

The grin disappeared from Ted's face, replaced by a quivering, sad smile.

"Two things. One was the creek turned into a trickle. Even desert cattle need water. I had to use CAP water to keep them alive."

It took Lilliana a few seconds to translate CAP to Central Arizona Project rather than something you wear on your head.

"The second was I got old."

"It happens to all of us," Lilliana said.

Ted nodded. "That it does. Ranching's a young man's game. My joints didn't take kindly to being in the saddle chasing cattle all day any more. My kids didn't inherit the ranching gene. They're off in Tucson and Phoenix working in offices. When Martha passed, the ranch house seemed much too big for one person."

And too full of memories, Lilliana wagered. Sometimes the memories were a comfort. Other times you had to leave them behind.

Ted straightened in his seat. "Anyway, when Russell Ellison came along and asked if I'd be interested in selling, I told him I might be, if the price was right. It was."

"But why didn't you just buy a house in town?" Lilliana asked. "Surely you don't need the income from the grocery."

"I've worked all my life. I tried sitting around. Watched too many game shows and reruns of Bonanza. I found out retirement is not for me, so I started looking around for some kind of business I could start. It dawned on me that people had to drive thirty miles when they ran out of milk. They'll still do that for their weekly shopping, but for the little things in between—I fill a need." Ted grinned again. "And I found out all you city slickers at the retirement home like to treat yourselves with things they don't serve in the dining room. It didn't take much to add those specialty items."

"You have no plans to retire?" Lilliana asked.

"None at all. I hope they find me laying on the floor of the store someday. I want to be stocking shelves right up to the very end."

Lilliana envied Ted Pulaski. She knew what he meant about feeling useful, having something to do every day that mattered. If it hadn't been for Charles's stroke, she'd still be a reference librarian, helping people learn about Shakespeare or history or astronomy or even African violets. But circumstances had dictated otherwise, and she'd retired long before she was ready. She sighed.

"Something wrong?" asked Ted.

"No, not really." But in her heart she wished her life had more purpose.

CHAPTER EIGHT

Lilliana walked up the lane leading to the retirement home at a pace significantly slower than usual. She'd been reluctant to leave the homey café and the pleasant conversation, but Ted had a store to run, and after an hour and a half, they'd reluctantly acknowledged it was time to leave. She felt that soft glow that comes from connecting to another person in a meaningful way. For the first time in over a year, she didn't feel alone in the world.

She'd have to go into town more often. Following the same routine, while comfortable, too easily became a limiting rut. Deeper than a rut. A trench. Maybe she should make an appointment at the hairdresser, change her hairstyle. Or stop by the knitting store and see if they carried embroidery floss or crewel patterns. She'd done quite a lot of embroidery before moving to Rainbow Ranch. A little outing every once in a while would be good for her. One that didn't involve seeing the chief of police.

It didn't take her long to reach the building. As she opened the door and stepped inside, the stuffiness of the air tried to smother her, and she realized she wanted to be outside where the gentle breeze could caress her face. A little nippy for swimming, but she could take a book out by the pool and read until dinner.

After putting the Styrofoam box containing the remains of her sandwich in the fridge, she picked up the book of Shakespeare sonnets she was reading and headed for the pool. As the warmth of a burgeoning spring washed over her, Lilliana didn't need the book to quote the sonnet that sang in her head.

Shall I compare thee to a summer's day?
Thou art more lovely and more temperate:
Rough winds do shake the darling buds of May,
(Or, in the case of Arizona, March, Lilliana amended)
And summer's lease hath all too short a date:

She was not the only one who had decided to enjoy the warm weather. Gathered around the pool were a dozen senior citizens. Several of her acquaintances had arranged their lounge chairs in a circle so they could talk.

"Mind if I join you?" Lilliana asked.

"Lily! Of course not." Lenny hopped up out of his seat and went to fetch another lounge chair. Frank moved his chair a little closer to Wayne, leaving room beside Mary for Lenny to put the additional chaise longue.

Before Lilliana totally settled in her chair Nancy asked, "Any news on the murder investigation?"

Five heads leaned in her direction. Wayne cupped his hand around his ear, the better to hear her response. Lilliana sighed. Of course they'd been discussing the murder. People's natural inclination was to be obsessed with the latest crisis or disaster —until they'd exhausted the topic fifty times over, or another train wreck occurred to take their attention off the first one. Personally, she'd enjoyed forgetting the unfortunate demise of Bette Tesselink over lunch with Ted. "No."

"Didn't you go into town to give your statement to the chief today?" Frank asked.

Lilliana nodded.

"Didn't he say anything?" Wayne asked.

"No."

"Come on, Lily, didn't you ask him about the investigation? Does he have any suspects?"

They really weren't going to let go of it, despite her one word answers. She might as well share her thoughts with them. Maybe one of her friends would come up with an idea. "To be honest," Lilliana said, "I don't think young Chief Cartwright knows what he's doing. I think this situation is beyond him."

Frank nodded sagely. "Doesn't surprise me."

"Why not?" Lilliana asked.

"The only reason he got the job is because he's Dale Ackerman's nephew," Frank said.

"I found that out today," Lilliana said. "But certainly he has some training?"

"Not much," Frank said. "I heard he was on the Tucson police force for three years, but I don't think he ever worked a homicide."

Lilliana recoiled at the sound of a piercing scream.

"EEE-YOW-OW!".

Mary, the one who'd shrieked so loudly, stared past Lilliana at a spot on the other side of the pool, her eyes wide with fear.

Lilliana turned and looked over her shoulder. A large black dog trotted toward them, tongue hanging out. It didn't look particularly menacing, but it certainly was big.

A black man sitting on the opposite side of the pool rose painfully from his chair with the help of a thick walking stick. He must have been six feet four or more and weigh over three hundred pounds. Maybe over four hundred. He took a few labored steps toward the dog and raised the walking stick over his head.

"Get!" he said in a loud, deep voice. "Go on! Get out of here!"

The dog stopped his progress toward the pool and looked at the man, evaluating the threat. The man shook his stick.

"I said GET!"

The dog cowered, turned, and ran back into the desert. Lilliana would have done the same thing. It wasn't only the size of the man. He projected a sense of presence, and man and beast alike would know not to mess with him.

"Say," Lenny said once the threat disappeared, "I have an idea."

Everyone turned their attention back to the conversation.

"What's that?" Lilliana asked.

"You should talk to Willie O'Mara. He was with TPD for thirty years. I'm pretty sure part of that time he was a detective. I'm sure he can give our young police chief some pointers."

"Who's Willie O'Mara?" Lilliana asked, puzzled.

"Him." Lenny pointed at the black man who'd shooed away the dog.

Lilliana turned and peered at the man again. He didn't look Irish.

* * *

"Excuse me," Lilliana said.

O'Mara, who had resumed reading his magazine, a science fiction one from the picture on the lurid cover, turned his head in Lilliana's direction. "How can I help you?"

"Would you mind if I asked you something?"

"Well, as long as it isn't anything terribly personal. I'm not going to tell you my cholesterol or blood sugar levels from my last physical."

What would make him think... oh. The smile on his face told Lilliana he'd been joking. She smiled weakly.

"Pull up a chair. I'd do it for you, but"—he gestured toward the walking stick lying across the bottom of the chaise.

Lilliana didn't physically have to pull up a chair. There was an empty one right next to him. Willie O'Mara had an odd sense of humor.

Once seated, she began. "Thank you."

"You're welcome."

The sound of water lapping against the sides of the pool intruded on the sudden silence. The group she'd just left gawked in her direction, eager for her to come back and tell them what happened. Which, so far, was nothing. And, judging by O'Mara's silence, would continue to be nothing unless she spoke up. "Lenny Rothenberg tells me you used to be a police officer."

"That's correct."

"I'm sure you heard about the murder of Bette Tesselink on Saturday?" She paused, hoping he'd say something indicating his willingness to discuss it with her.

He just nodded.

It appeared as if she was going to have to carry this conversation herself. "I've been talking with Chief Cartwright, and to be honest, I think he's in over his head."

More silence. A stony stare. Maybe this hadn't been such a good idea.

She persevered. "I was wondering if you might talk to him, give him some pointers, so we can resolve this speedily."

"Are you a friend of Mr. Ellison?"

Lilliana was taken aback, not only by the question, but by the fact that he'd spoken at all. "Why would you think that?"

O'Mara blinked and settled back into his chair. "Because he has the most to lose if this place gets a deadly reputation. How many folks will want to live in a retirement community where people are murdered in broad daylight?"

He had a point. Lilliana was compelled to add, "Actually, I might have the most to lose. Chief Cartwright—and Russ Ellison—seem to think I'm the murderer. You see, I had an argument with Bette shortly before she was killed. I might have lost my temper a little bit, but I certainly didn't want to kill her."

Lilliana licked lips suddenly gone dry. "And, uh, the murder weapon was my softball bat."

"Puts you in kind of a pickle, doesn't it?" O'Mara brushed at a leaf blown onto his slacks from the nearby mesquite trees. "So did you?"

"Did I what?" Horrified once she realized what he meant, she hastened to add, "Oh, no." She'd already told him she didn't want to kill Bette. Why would he be asking? And why would he be staring at her like that?

"I don't think you did," O'Mara said. "I can generally tell

when a person is lying. There are things they teach you, body language and such, that give people away even if they think they're controlling themselves. You didn't do any of those things."

"See, that proves you'd be perfect to help Chief Cartwright."

O'Mara closed his eyes for a minute. Lilliana didn't know whether he was napping or thinking. As it turned out, he'd been thinking.

"I'm not sure that's such a good idea," O'Mara said after opening his eyes. He ticked off the reasons on his fingers. "One: I was his superior in Tucson. If I horn in on his investigation, he might not do as good a job as he could do without my being there. He'll stop trying to solve the murder himself. Two: He'll lose credibility in the town. When you're a police officer, particularly if you're the chief, it's very important that the citizens trust you. Without trust, your job is almost impossible. I have a feeling young Chad Cartwright has enough problems in that area. Three: I have no authority to do that. I'm retired."

Lilliana was filled with dismay. Visions of being arrested, tried, and convicted with no more than circumstantial evidence played in her head. "But how will the murder be solved?"

O'Mara gave her an appraising look. "You appear to be a very capable woman."

Lilliana nodded. "Yes. Generally."

"And you've already spoken to Chief Cartwright several times."

"That's right." *What was he getting at?*

"I have an idea. I can't help Chief Cartwright directly because of all the reasons I stated. But you, you're just an old woman—pardon me for putting it that way—and it would be natural for you to try to help the young man out. So suppose I give you a few ideas. Then you devise an opportunity to suggest those to our chief of police at the appropriate time. He wouldn't feel threatened by you, the town would never assume you're integral to the investigation, and we find the real murderer."

What an interesting idea, thought Lilliana. It certainly sounded more interesting than embroidery. "I'll do it."

CHAPTER NINE

Shirley's cleaning cart was stopped outside her apartment when Lilliana went back inside to tend to her African violets. Housekeeping was one of the perks of living in a retirement community. While Lilliana had no problem with washing dishes for the few meals she ate here instead of in the dining room, or wiping down countertops afterwards, it was a pleasure to have someone else do all the dusting and vacuuming and cleaning of toilets.

Shirley was wiping out the inside of the microwave when Lilliana entered.

"So nice to see you, Shirley."

The middle-aged black woman turned from her task. "Nice to see you again, too, Ms. Wentworth. I'll be out of your way in just a few minutes."

"No hurry. Take your time to finish up."

Lilliana headed down the hallway to put the book of sonnets on her bedside table so she could read it before she went to sleep. She never had gotten around to opening the book at the pool. As she put the book down, she saw the missing button from Saturday lying beside the lamp. Shirley must have found it when she vacuumed. Lilliana picked it up and went back to the kitchen.

She held up the button and said, "Thanks for finding this. I couldn't imagine where it had fallen off."

Shirley looked puzzled. "I didn't find that button. I saw it on the night table when I was dusting and figured you just hadn't had time to sew it back on."

Hmmm. Lilliana was quite sure she hadn't put the button on the table. Or was that something else she'd forgotten? She fretted over that for a minute. No, she was certain. She hadn't put the button on the table. *How did it get there?*

Had someone been inside her apartment today while she was out? That was a discomforting thought. She always locked the door, both when she left and when she was home. Although she'd never heard of any thefts at Rainbow Ranch or any other criminal activity—until Bette's murder, of course—she was cautious by nature. She certainly didn't know all the residents or staff, and there were always visitors around as well.

Lilliana glanced around the living room, then went back to her bedroom. She checked her jewelry box, verified the lockbox was still hidden at the back of her closet, and scanned the clothes hanging inside. As far as she could tell, nothing had been taken. That made her feel a little better, but she still didn't like the idea of someone being in her apartment.

She heard Shirley shut the door on her way out and hurried to check that she'd locked the door behind her. She had. Shirley was reliable. She had to take Shirley's word for it that she hadn't found the button.

But if it hadn't been Shirley, who put the button on her nightstand?

* * *

Lilliana had agreed to meet Willie O'Mara in the library after dinner to discuss their strategy. While the room saw frequent use during the day between people looking for books to read and meetings of the various groups, it was rarely occupied in the evening, most residents preferring to watch television then.

Lilliana loved this room, not only for the books, which, of course, as a former librarian were of great importance to her, but for its homey feel. In addition to the two chairs in front of the windows at the far corner, there were easy chairs in two other corners, overstuffed and covered in floral fabrics, and plenty of reading lamps to provide good light. If you removed the conference table from the center, it could almost be a room in someone's home. It stood in sharp contrast to the other public rooms in the retirement community, which all had an institutional look about them.

O'Mara sat in one of the two large easy chairs farthest from the entrance. He looked up from the book he was reading as she walked in. "Glad you came."

Lilliana crossed the room and took the other chair. "Did you think I wouldn't?"

She glanced at the cover of the book in his hands. A Joseph Wambaugh, appropriate enough for a former police officer.

"No. You seem like the dependable type to me." He closed the book and put it on the occasional table between them.

This time Lilliana didn't wait for O'Mara, but launched into a series of questions. "So where should we start? Do you think we can get the list of evidence that was collected? Or find out if there were any fingerprints left behind that would give away the killer?"

"That's unlikely, although in a town as small as this one, they may not obey the rules quite as closely. Even if they got great fingerprints from the crime scene, you have to have a suspect to match those prints to. I doubt the chief would let us examine the evidence. Although the file would be helpful, most crimes are solved by interviewing people, finding out what they know, and putting the pieces together."

Lilliana frowned. The most obvious fingerprints on the softball bat were bound to be hers. It was not in her best interest to bring that up. "Do you have any suggestions?"

O'Mara shook his head. "I didn't know the victim. I'd seen her around, of course, but I never spoke to her. You did, though. Is there anyone you can think of who had a problem with her?" He stared intently at Lilliana, making her a bit uncomfortable.

"The problem with Bette Tesselink is nobody liked her. She was a pro at creating problems with other people. She complained about the housekeeping staff. They never cleaned her apartment to her satisfaction, and she expected them to do things—like wash windows—that aren't in the agreement. She complained about Miguel, too. She thought he took too long to fix her running toilet. I'm pretty sure she complained about the meals."

"But do you think she made any of the staff angry enough to kill her?" O'Mara asked.

Lilliana sighed. "No."

"Still," O'Mara said, "it might be worthwhile to talk to them. If Bette Tesselink was as good at pushing people's buttons as you've led me to believe, it's possible one of them reacted more strongly than you think they did."

"I'll have to suggest that to Chief Cartwright."

"I've been thinking about that, too," O'Mara said. "If he's any kind of a cop, and I think he is despite his inexperience, he's probably already talked to them once. But, since you appear to be the prime suspect, he might not have questioned them as thoroughly as he should have."

Lilliana bristled at what she took as an accusation. "As I told that young chief of police, Frank Bellandini, who told me she'd stolen his hybrid and was showing it as her own, was as angry as I was."

"Easy there. I wasn't saying I think you *are* the prime suspect. I said you appear to be. And certainly Frank Bellandini has to be on our list of possibles. My point was I've been thinking that rather than trying to tell Chief Cartwright how to run his investigation, it would be better to do our own and then present him with what we've found out."

O'Mara's idea sounded like a bit more involvement than Lilliana had expected. But she saw his point. "So maybe I should start by talking to Frank a bit."

The former police detective nodded. "Wouldn't be a bad idea. And the other members of your club. I'll talk to Ellison and see what I can find out from him."

"That sounds like a good plan, Mr. O'Mara," Lilliana said.

"Willie," O'Mara corrected. "Please call me Willie, Mrs. Wentworth."

"And you must call me Lilliana," she replied.

"Of course, Lilliana. Shall we meet back here tomorrow evening and compare notes?"

* * *

As Lilliana rounded the corner on the way to her apartment, she noticed the door to the clinic was open. Kirstie, the nurse, stood inside. That reminded her that she was almost out of the Aleve she sometimes took for the arthritis in her knees, particularly after a softball game. She rapped lightly on the door and entered the clinic.

It was a small room, with a desk positioned opposite the door, a scale beside it, and a chair for the patient to sit in. An examining table filled most of the space, while a counter with cabinets overhead covered the wall beside the door.

Kirstie stood at the counter, where about a dozen prescription containers were lined up, split into two groups. A young woman in her twenties, she was best known for riding a Harley-Davidson to work. She looked up as Lilliana entered and put down the pen with which she'd been making notations on a form on her clipboard. "Good evening, Mrs. Wentworth."

"Good evening, Kirstie. Working late this evening?"

Kirstie nodded. "Mr. Ellison wanted me to pick up the medications from Mrs. Tesselink's casita, so after I gave out the evening meds, I went and got them. I think he was afraid someone might take them. If anyone got ill from taking her meds, that would be a big liability for the retirement community." She held up the clipboard. "I have to make a record before disposing of them."

"Those are all Bette's?" Lilliana's eyes widened, and she bent her head closer as she tried to read the labels.

Kirstie pushed back a long wisp of blonde hair that had escaped the knot at the nape of her neck and fallen in front of her face. "Uh huh." Her expression changed to one of concern. "Only I shouldn't tell you that. Privacy rules, you know."

"Fiddle! Bette's dead. How can you violate the privacy of someone who's dead?"

Kirstie contemplated this, then leaned forward conspiratorially. "I guess you're right. Most of the residents here take a lot of medications. You're the unusual one. Generally, someone as healthy as you are doesn't decide to live in a place like this. They stay on their own."

Pain stabbed Lilliana's heart. If it hadn't been for Charles, she probably wouldn't be here. She pushed that thought aside and focused on Bette Tesselink. "What kinds of medicines was she taking?"

"Oh, the usual," Kirstie said casually. "Blood pressure, diuretic, a statin for her cholesterol, Avandia."

"What's Avandia?" Lilliana asked.

"It's for diabetes. Something you wouldn't have to worry about." Kirstie appraised Lilliana's athletic form.

Lilliana was disappointed. She'd hoped there might be some other drug, something that might be a clue. She spoke her thoughts. "So nothing unusual? She didn't have any disease or anything? Maybe something that would explain her nasty behavior?"

Kirstie laughed. "No. I guess her behavior was just the way she was. Now there are others here, like Mr. Rothenberg, who do take some strange things."

Lilliana's ears perked up. "Like what?"

"Wait, I shouldn't have said that." Kirstie looked worried. Swept up in the conversation, she'd apparently forgotten about confidentiality.

"Nevermind," Lilliana said. "I shouldn't have asked you. And don't worry, I won't say anything."

"Thank you." Kirstie's face cleared. "Was there something you needed?"

Lilliana got her Aleve and headed back to her apartment. She just might make a visit to Lenny's apartment tomorrow and see what she could see.

CHAPTER TEN

Lilliana was up with the sun the next morning. What with the African Violet Club show and the murder, three days had gone by since she'd last gotten any exercise, if you didn't count her walk into town. And she missed it. She doubted there would be a softball practice soon; she still hadn't convinced enough of the residents to join the team, not to mention the loss of her bat. She didn't care for tai chi or tennis or the machines in the exercise room, although she used the latter when the temperature was too high or monsoon storms threatened. She preferred to take a vigorous walk, usually in the morning before breakfast.

The retirement community had constructed a maze of paved walking paths that led out from the front door, around the south wing, the pool, and the casitas, and continued a short way into the desert behind the buildings. Multiple paths threaded their way through saguaro and prickly pear cactus. In a few places, a small recess beside the path, with a stone bench and some flowering plants or a bird feeder, provided a spot where, if you got tired—which wasn't unusual for many of the residents—you could have a seat, rest, and enjoy the view.

That's the way Lilliana usually went in the morning, but today she decided to walk on the other side of the facility, out in the wild desert. That was for two reasons. One was the big, black dog that had approached them at the pool the other day. The dog had gone back into the desert on the swimming pool side. Lilliana wouldn't be surprised if one of the residents had been misguidedly feeding it. A lot of them missed their pets, and while many retirement homes in Tucson allowed residents to have animals, Rainbow Ranch didn't.

The second reason was that she wanted to see if she could find the pond Ted had told her about. With so little moisture, water in the desert attracted people like a magnet pulled iron filings. Any chance to be near open water was a treat.

She strode by the tennis courts on the northwest side of the complex, waving at Lenny as she passed. He was tossing balls in the air, practicing his serve. He also had trouble getting people to participate in sports. Lilliana briefly thought about switching from softball to tennis just to have someone to play with on a regular basis, but quickly banished that thought from her mind. It was too likely that Lenny would take her interest in exercise as an interest in him.

It amazed her how much like high school the retirement facility was. Little romances sprang up all the time. Jealousies over who sat next to whom at the Friday night movies. Gossip about chaste kisses exchanged in the gazebo. After being married to Charles for over forty years, Lilliana had no desire for the casual flings the other senior citizens engaged in.

Ahead lay an expanse of rock-strewn desert. No paved paths

led where she was going. She stepped carefully, having more than once been tripped up by the odd stone underfoot, resulting in scraped knees and elbows. She didn't heal as quickly as she used to and had no desire to be sporting scabbed hands at mealtime.

However, as she picked her way through the clear spots, she noticed that there was something like a path, long unused, leading back into the foothills. Perhaps this had been how Ted and his family had gone to the natural spring in the past. Reassured by this thought, Lilliana quickened her pace, pushing her heart rate up and forcing her lungs to work harder. Going uphill added to the strenuousness of her walk, but she was fit and didn't mind stretching her limits.

The plant growth became more dense as she moved away from the land where the retirement community had been built. Creosote bushes and clumps of native grasses joined the cacti on either side of the path, blocking her view of her immediate surroundings. She could still see the mountains, of course, and the roof of the retirement home, but she felt like she was leaving civilization behind for the wilderness of an older Arizona.

A family of quail, the chicks no bigger than darning eggs, scurried out of the brush on one side, across the path, and quickly disappeared on the other side. This time of day, there were plenty of birds calling to one another as they greeted the morning. She surprised a rabbit when she took a turn around a particularly large creosote bush. The rabbit froze in place for a moment before loping off into the desert and out of sight.

Distracted by the movement of the animal, only after the rabbit was gone was her gaze drawn to the muddy pool on the opposite side. She'd found it. The pool was smaller than Lilliana had expected, maybe fifteen feet wide by thirty feet long. A rim of dried mud showed that it swelled to possibly twice its current size during monsoon season. The water didn't look very deep. She couldn't imagine that it had ever served to water a herd of cattle, but Ted had said the pool was bigger when he was a boy.

Vegetation huddled around the water, including a few desert willow trees near the far end of the pond. Trees were so rare in Arizona, especially ones with the beautiful flowers of the desert willow in the summer, Lilliana was drawn to them as strongly as she was to the water. She would have to come back to this spot in May or June to enjoy the blooms. As she approached the trees, she was able to see the small stream that fed the pond. Unlike the pond, the stream was clear and sparkled in the mottled sunlight under the leaves of the willows. Lilliana squatted and dipped her fingers in the water. It was icy cold—at least compared to the warmth of the air.

She followed the stream back, wondering if she could find its source, or if it was far up the hillside, higher than she was willing to climb today. The stream twisted and turned as it made its way through the rocky ground, finding the path of least resistance. She circled a particularly large willow tree and came upon a widening in the stream caused by an eddy around the roots. On the opposite side was the strangest bird Lilliana had ever seen. Its breast appeared to be flesh colored, while the wings were a bright yellow. It almost looked like…

The bird hovered over a cholla cactus, plucking buds from its branches. *Plucking?*

Birds didn't pluck. Except with their beaks. Lilliana was quite sure the bird wasn't using its beak. And the fluttering wings didn't look like bird wings. They were more like butterfly wings, waving over the creature's back then forward over its... arms?

She shook her head. Surely her imagination was running away with her. If only she could get closer, she was sure she'd see what strange pattern of coloring was causing the humanizing effect. But before Lilliana could cross the stream and get close enough to see the bird clearly, it spotted her and flew off up the hillside.

Lilliana hurried after the bird, anxious to take a closer look at it, but she was slowed by the difficult terrain. Each time she thought she caught a glimpse of the yellow wings, the bird darted off again. While the bird could fly in a straight line, Lilliana had to zig and zag around the rocks and the stream and the vegetation. She circled a gnarled ironwood tree. She was panting and thinking of giving up the chase when she came upon a second pond, slightly smaller than the first one, but filled with crystal clear water just begging to be drunk.

Which it was, by a herd of javelina not ten feet in front of her. You didn't have to live in Arizona long before learning about javelina, an animal that looked like a mutant pig, not pink like a real pig, but gray or black with an overly large head. It was a small herd, only seven animals, but Lilliana had no desire to tangle with them. She started to back away, but it was too late. One had seen her and let out a squeal of alarm.

The muttering and snorting sounds they'd been making as they drank at the pond stopped, giving way to more squeals, snorts, and loud popping noises, and the herd began to scatter in all directions. The largest one, the one who had first seen her and trumpeted the alarm, headed toward her, mouth open to expose long, sharp teeth.

Lilliana turned to run, but knew that she'd never outpace the animal in the rocky terrain. The trees presented another obstacle.

Or salvation.

Remembering the ironwood, she ran toward it, retracing her steps until she reached the only tree sturdy enough to support her weight. It had been close to fifty years since Lilliana had last climbed a tree, but she had a lot of motivation at the moment. The thud of hooves grew closer. She ignored the jabs from the spines of the baby saguaros beneath its branches as she ran to the trunk. She leapt and caught hold of a low-hanging branch with her right hand and grasped the trunk with her left, clinging to it for all she was worth. Putting her feet on the trunk below her, she pushed up until she could reach the branch with her left hand as well. It took all her strength—and the surge of adrenalin coursing through her veins—to pull herself up on top of it. For the moment, she was safe.

But below her, the javelina circled, chuffing and snorting and waiting for his breakfast.

Her skin dried quickly in the arid air as her heart rate slowed, and her breathing calmed from gasps to measured breaths. She sat very still on the branch, knowing the eyesight of javelinas wasn't very sharp, and hoped he wouldn't smell the sweat coating her body. She could certainly smell him. The strong, musky odor threatened to choke her.

Twenty minutes later, the javelina lost interest in Lilliana and wandered off, snuffling through the vegetation.

When she was sure it wasn't coming back, she looked down

and estimated how many feet it was to the ground. Maybe five or six. Still too far to take in one jump. She turned and grasped the trunk, hugging it like a lover, and stretched her foot in a pointe position as memories of childhood ballet classes came back to her. Her toes searched for the lower branch.

Once she touched the rough surface, she tried to look down over her shoulder, but couldn't see much while hugging the ironwood tree. She tapped her foot a few times, gauging the width of the branch and where the center was. Once she had determined the strongest place for her right foot, she repeated the process with her left foot.

Lilliana took a deep breath, then slowly lowered her weight onto the branch as she slid her arms down the bark of the trunk. She winced as bits of skin scraped off her palms, but held on until she rested securely on the lower branch. Looking down, she was now only three feet off the ground. Close enough. She bent her knees until she was squatting, let go of the trunk to grasp the branch with both hands, then dropped her feet to the ground. She felt a twinge in her ankle, but other than that, she was in one piece.

So much for her little adventure of the morning. She'd better get back. Lenny was surely done with his tennis practice and at breakfast by now. She didn't want to miss her chance to start her investigation.

CHAPTER ELEVEN

Lilliana entered the dining room, having showered, put on clean clothes, and hoping she wasn't too late. She exhaled as she spotted Lenny, Mary, and Nancy dawdling over coffee in the dining room.

"Well, good morning sleepy head," Mary said as she stirred a spoonful of sugar into her cup.

"I thought you got up early," Nancy said. "I'm the one who is always late for breakfast." Evidencing this, scrambled eggs and toast remained on the plate in front of her.

"I *was* up early." Lilliana craned her neck, looking for a waitress to bring hot water for her tea. As usual, she'd brought her own Earl Grey teabags since the retirement home only served Lipton.

"I can attest to that," Lenny said. "I saw her heading out for a walk this morning. Where'd you go that you're only getting back now?"

"Ted told me about a stream that runs in back of the retirement home property, and I went to find it."

"Ted?" Mary asked with a sly glance in Lilliana's direction.

She felt her face redden. "Ted Pulaski. The owner of the grocery store."

"I didn't know about any stream." Lenny sipped from his glass of orange juice. Lenny never drank anything containing caffeine—no coffee or tea or even hot chocolate. He claimed caffeine wasn't good for you. Lilliana didn't know about that, but she'd take her chances. Starting her day without tea wouldn't be starting the day at all.

"Did you find it?" Nancy leaned forward eagerly. "I used to go fishing with my father when I was a little girl. We'd spend all day at the river. Sometimes we went to a lake. Mamma would fry up the fish we caught for breakfast. I'd love some fried fish. All they serve here is plain, baked, white fish. It doesn't taste like anything." She wrinkled her nose.

The waitress had come back into the dining room carrying a fresh pan of scrambled eggs for the buffet table. Lilliana caught her attention and waved her over. Once her teacup was filled, she rose and said, "I'm going to get some of those eggs while they're still hot. I'll tell you about the stream in a minute."

While scooping scrambled eggs onto her plate, Lilliana thought about how to tell the tale of this morning's adventure. Her inclination was to minimize it. If she mentioned the attack of the javelina, Russ Ellison was bound to make some rule about not going hiking off the paved trails. What fun would that be? Life in Rainbow Ranch was too calm for her taste as it was. She'd felt more alive since the unfortunate events of last weekend than she had the whole time she'd lived here. A lump rose in her throat, and Lilliana berated herself for even thinking about Bette Tesselink's murder that way.

On the other hand, it might be fun to exaggerate her adventure and see everyone's expression. She should leave out the part about the bird, though. If she told them she thought it might not have been a bird, might, in fact, have been something out of a children's story, there was a good chance someone would mention it to Kirstie. Or, worse, Russ Ellison. She had no desire to go through a psychiatric evaluation.

Once she'd finished dishing out her portion of eggs, she took a slice of dry wheat toast and a packet of strawberry jam and headed back to the table.

"So did you find the stream?" Nancy asked.

"As a matter of fact, I did." Lilliana opened the packet of jam and spread it on her toast.

Nancy leaned forward. "Where is it? Are there fish in the stream?"

Lilliana cut the piece of toast in half, put one half on her plate and took a small bite out of the other. She swallowed, then said, "I didn't notice."

"How could you not notice?" Nancy asked.

Lenny put a hand on Nancy's arm. "I don't think she ever went fishing."

Lilliana shook her head and realized what an amazing statement that was. In seventy years, she had never baited a hook, never held a fishing rod in her hand, never wrangled a fish out of the water. It seemed like something one should do once. She'd have to put "go fishing" on her bucket list.

"So where is this hidden stream?" Lenny asked.

"It's not hidden," Lilliana replied as she scooped up some eggs on her fork. Before putting the eggs in her mouth, she said, "It's off to the northwest, behind the tennis courts."

Mary, who had been quiet, asked wistfully, "Could I get there with my walker?"

"I'm afraid not," Lilliana said and felt sorry for Mary. "The ground is uneven, quite rocky in places as a matter of fact. The stream ends in a muddy little pond not too far from here." For some reason, she was reluctant to talk about the clear pool farther up the mountain.

Nancy perked up at this statement. "Are there fish in the pond? I think a breading made with anise and coriander would be delicious on fried fish fillets."

Lilliana made an effort to not make a face. Licorice-flavored fish didn't sound at all appetizing to her. "There was too much mud in the water to see.

"I did come upon the oddest bird, though. The coloring was amazing. Its underside was flesh-colored, and the wings were lemon yellow," Lilliana continued before she remembered she wasn't going to talk about that. "I tried to follow it, but I ran into a herd of javelina."

Mary gasped. "Javelina! You could have been killed!"

Lilliana realized she had shared a bit too much of her story. Between the dog and the javelina herd, it was a sure bet Ellison would issue a dictate about no walking on the grounds at all. "No, no. Javelina aren't really dangerous. They just get excited too easily. I didn't have a problem with them at all." She wondered if there was a Presbyterian equivalent of confession for sinners, because telling that lie certainly had to count as a sin. She thought she'd better cover her bases on the presence of the javelina. "Let's not mention the herd to any of the staff."

Lenny, knowing the results of such a communication as well

as Lilliana did, said, "I agree. There's no need for Ellison to know anything about the javelina. Or the pond and stream. Let's keep that to ourselves."

Mary was already nodding, but Nancy didn't look quite so sure. "But they could be dangerous. Although I would like to go fishing."

"I'll make you a deal," Lenny said to Nancy. "You don't say anything to Ellison, and I'll take you fishing tomorrow."

Nancy's face brightened at that. "Would you? That would be wonderful!" Then her face fell. "But I don't have a fishing pole."

"Maybe we can find one at the drug store," Lenny said. "I'll take a walk into town after breakfast and check."

"You are so good to me." Nancy gazed at Lenny with cow eyes, her version of flirting. She looked so ridiculous, Lilliana had to cover her mouth with her napkin to keep everyone from seeing her choking back laughter.

Willie O'Mara entered the dining room and turned his head from side to side, obviously searching for someone. When he spotted Lilliana, he headed in her direction, walking more slowly and leaning more heavily on his walking stick than Lilliana remembered him doing before. When he arrived, he asked, "Lilliana, could I have a word with you?"

His eyes went to the others at the table, and Lilliana understood he meant alone. Just as she was going to suggest she meet him in the library in a little while, Lenny rose from his seat and said, "I think I'm going to go into town now. Would you like to join me, Nancy?"

Nancy blushed. "I'd love to."

Lilliana realized that, if Lenny were going into town, she'd have to wait to question him. Not wanting to wait any longer than necessary, she quickly said, "Lenny? Today is watering day, and I realized this morning that I'm all out of plant food. Would you be able to lend me some?"

"Sure, Lily. I'll bring it to lunch."

"Oh, you don't have to bother. I'll stop by your apartment around 11:30, if that's all right. Do you think you'll be back by then?"

Lenny smiled at Nancy. "Probably. The drug store isn't that big. If I'm not there, just figure I've gone fishing, and we'll arrange another time."

"Thank you so much," Lilliana said.

"I should be going, too." Mary pushed herself up out of her chair and reached for her walker. "See you at lunch."

Lilliana watched Mary roll herself out of the dining room, while Willie settled himself heavily in the chair next to her. "Oof."

"Are you all right?"

"I'm fine," Willie said. "It's my hip. Too many years riding around in a patrol car. Some days are better than others. I really need a hip replacement, but my doctor wants me to lose fifty pounds first." He grimaced, whether at the idea of going on a diet or from the pain in his hip, Lilliana wasn't sure. His yellow knit shirt did seem stretched to its limit over his ample stomach.

"It's hard to lose weight without exercising," Lilliana said, "but it can be done. All you have to do is eat less. Have salad instead of potatoes and skip dessert." Her voice carried the conviction of the naturally thin.

Willie smiled. "You sound like my doctor. Only I grew up

eating potatoes every day. It's the Irish in me."

Lilliana didn't want to be rude, but he looked more like Othello than Macmorris, the only Irish character in Shakespeare's plays. She had to ask. "The Irish?"

Willie's smile turned into a grin, and he laughed out loud. "Gotcha, didn't I? Well, it's true. My mother was African-American and my father was Irish. Makes me true Black Irish." He chuckled.

Lilliana had heard the term Black Irish before, but wasn't sure it meant what Willie was implying it did. She'd have to look it up later. Regardless, Willie thought it was funny, so she smiled back at him. "What did you want to talk to me about?"

Willie's face turned serious at that point. "I got a chance to talk to Ellison this morning."

"Yes," Lilliana dragged out the word, encouraging him to say more.

"Of course, first I got a bunch of 'how terrible' and 'bad for the retirement community' and that sort of thing. Not useful. We already know how sensitive Ellison is about bad press. But I just let him blather. A lot of times people will say more if you don't interrupt them." Willie paused. "Ellison did."

"What did he say?" Lilliana was getting as impatient as Nancy had been. Willie seemed to be enjoying making her wait.

"He said, and I quote, 'She never got to tell me what she knew.' He seemed very frustrated. Then he mumbled something about 'worth a fortune.' When I asked him to repeat it, he looked alarmed, like he'd forgotten he wasn't just talking to himself and said, 'Nevermind.' He hurried off to his office then."

"That *is* interesting," Lilliana said. Her heart was beating faster. A real clue! Maybe someone else knew what Bette had been going to divulge and was hoping to cash in on him—or her—self. "I wonder what she was going to tell him."

"I have no idea." Willie hung his head. "I must have lost my touch."

"Oh, I doubt that very much. But if there really was something Bette found out that was worth money, someone else might have known about it, too, and hoped to take advantage of it. I wonder what Bette knew."

CHAPTER TWELVE

Lilliana considered what she should do with the next couple of hours. Willie was going to have another go at Ellison later today and see if he could get more information from him. Lenny and Nancy wouldn't be back from town until almost lunch time. She doubted the likelihood of Mary's involvement in the murder.

She wondered if there was anything in Bette's casita that would tell her what Ellison had been referring to when he slipped and told Willie she knew something worth a fortune. Lilliana doubted it. Ellison had probably gone and looked himself right after Bette had died. But maybe he missed something.

Bette had a daughter, Susan, if Lilliana remembered correctly, who lived in Tucson, but she doubted Susan had come out to collect her mother's things yet. Even though Bette was such a pain in the butt, Lilliana had felt sorry for her when she found out Bette's daughter only came out to visit once a month. If that. Although Bette's incessant complaining tended to exaggerate the facts, it seemed as if Susan didn't want to be bothered with her mother. Bette had asked her to come more often, but she always had some excuse. And Susan never seemed to remember to bring Bette the little things she liked: her favorite brand of shampoo instead of the one supplied by the retirement home, a box of chocolates, some perfume.

But she didn't think it would be too long before Susan cleared out Bette's casita. If Lilliana wanted to search it for clues, time was of the essence. Perhaps this morning she could figure out a way to get inside. It was worth a chance.

The casitas stood behind the main building, with the pool and tennis courts in between. The front entrances of the single-story homes faced the courtyard, and private patios overlooked the mountains to the rear. Lilliana had gone through one before she moved in. She would have liked the privacy, but the individual units cost too much for her pension.

Bette had occupied the end one behind the swimming pool, so Lilliana followed the walking path around the pool, where several residents were doing water aerobics with an instructor who came up from Benson twice a week. If Lilliana wasn't able to find more players for the softball team, she was going to have to think about signing up for some of the physical fitness classes. Doing so would also have the benefit of letting her meet some of the other residents. Other than the members of the African Violet Club—and now Willie—she hadn't gotten to know many people here. Since it looked as if she'd be spending the rest of her life at Rainbow Ranch, she probably should think about broadening her social contacts.

She approached the door of Bette's casita and, after checking to make sure no one was around, tried the handle.

She should have known the door would be locked. The living room window was closed and, Lilliana was sure, locked from inside as well. Besides, she'd be in view of the pool and anyone passing by if she attempted to crawl in a window. That included not only the residents, but Kirstie dispensing medications, Shirley coming to attend to the housekeeping tasks, Miguel fixing dripping faucets or running toilets, and Russell Ellison, who wouldn't be doing anything useful, but often popped up at unexpected moments.

There was another way.

Once again checking to make sure no one was watching her, Lilliana circled around the rear of the building to try the sliding glass door to the patio. She was just about to climb over the railing when she noticed a wisp of smoke out of the corner of her eye. *Was something burning?*

Lilliana turned quickly, ready to telephone the fire department, and saw Frank Bellandini standing back near a saguaro cactus, a cigarette in his hand. He wore a green plaid shirt, and his knobby knees stuck out beneath a pair of khaki shorts.

Their eyes met, each gauging the other, evaluating what the response would be. Never one to back down, Lilliana held his gaze as she walked toward him deliberately.

Frank raised the cigarette to his lips and inhaled. He held the smoke in his lungs for the few moments it took Lilliana to reach him, then let it out slowly. The ritual reminded her of the sixties, an aging hippy smoking a joint. Except the smell was clearly of tobacco, not marijuana.

"Good morning, Lilliana. I thought you took your constitutional before breakfast."

"I do." She waited for him to say something else. After at least a minute had passed, she waited no longer. "I didn't know you smoked."

Frank gave her a crooked smile. "You're not supposed to. No one is." He furtively glanced around, checking for anyone else in the area.

Smoking was forbidden on the grounds of Rainbow Ranch. Not only was it unhealthy for the smoker and those around him, it was a fire hazard. With so many disabled people, a fire could be a disaster, since they might not be able to escape a burning building on their own. Lilliana took a glance over her shoulder. Frank and his cigarette would be clearly visible from the patio door of Bette's casita. She wondered if he'd had another smoking place, one more secluded, when Bette was alive.

"I hope you're not going to be as much of a nuisance as Bette," Frank said as if reading her mind. "She kept threatening to tell Ellison I was smoking on the grounds. What harm am I doing anyone but myself?" He rubbed the back of his neck.

"And that isn't enough? I thought everyone had quit by now. I'm sure you could get Kirstie to give you some nicotine gum or get you those patches or something."

Frank took another drag on his cigarette, then dropped the filter on the ground and ground it under his heel. "I like smoking. It relaxes me."

Lilliana stared at the butt, flattened and mixed with the sandy soil of the Arizona desert. "It's also a fire hazard. And litter."

"I'm careful. You saw how I put it out. And I'll take the remains with me when I leave. Toss them in the Dumpster before I go back to my apartment. What difference does it make to you?"

"I believe in following the rules," she said firmly. In truth, Lilliana wasn't sure Frank's smoking was a big deal. She didn't approve of it, but as long as he smoked away from everyone else and was careful not to start a fire, why shouldn't he have the pleasure? Lilliana could imagine how she'd react if someone decided to make a rule against Earl Grey tea. She would probably smuggle it in anyway. "I suppose you're not doing anyone any harm."

The tension went out of Frank's body. Apparently he'd been more concerned than he'd let on. "Good. I'm glad you're being more reasonable than Bette. She even hinted she could be persuaded not to tell anyone if I gave her a little present every once in a while. I pretended I didn't understand what she was talking about, but she'd gotten more insistent lately. It sounded like she was short of money."

"Oh? I thought her husband left her a fairly large inheritance. That's why she could afford to live in a casita instead of an apartment."

Frank shrugged. "Got me. All I know is what she said."

That certainly gave Lilliana something to think about.

"Ready to go back now?" Frank asked.

Reluctantly, Lilliana nodded. There was no way she could try the patio doors to Bette's casita with Frank watching her.

Frank bent over and picked up the crushed cigarette butt. "So how did you do at the sale this past weekend?" he asked as they walked back toward the building. "I sold quite a few plants and leaves myself."

"So did I," Lilliana said. Bringing up the sale reminded her of Ted. She wondered if she'd see him again. Other than to buy tea that is. "I hope we also stirred up some interest in the retirement home. We really need more than ten members if we want to be a real club."

"When's the next meeting?" Frank asked. A breeze ruffled his thinning gray hair.

"Thursday, in the library. I thought we should talk about our next event and start making plans for it."

Frank raised his eyebrows. "So soon?"

Lilliana chuckled. "Sarah and I thought the meeting should be right after the show so people who were thinking about joining wouldn't forget. Most of us have at least a touch of old timer's disease."

Frank smiled in return. "Ah, yes. I've been known to have a senior moment or two of my own. How about I make up some flyers on my computer and put them around the place? You know, on the bulletin board in the library, on the door to the TV room, wherever. Maybe put one on every table in the dining room at breakfast tomorrow morning. Try to drum up some interest."

"Why, Frank, that's a terrific idea. I should have thought of it myself."

"You don't have the background. Running a restaurant, I learned to take advantage of every minute to promote the business. Librarians don't do that."

Lilliana conceded the point. By this time they'd reached the end of the casitas. As they turned the corner toward the front, Lilliana saw Shirley's cleaning cart parked outside Bette's unit. The door yawned open.

CHAPTER THIRTEEN

After spying Shirley's cart, Lilliana decided this might be the perfect opportunity for her to get inside. "You go ahead without me, Frank. I need to talk to Shirley about getting my carpet spot-cleaned. Sometimes I'm a bit clumsy when I'm watering."

Frank nodded. "I know how that is. And you don't realize you've dripped until you see the dirt spot later on. I'll catch you later, Lilliana."

"Don't forget about those flyers," she called out as Frank headed for the swimming pool.

She stepped around the cart and rapped lightly on the open door. "Shirley?"

Shirley's friendly face popped out from behind a wall. "Oh, it's you, Ms. Wentworth. What can I do for you?"

Lilliana stepped into the casita, glancing from side to side to see the state of things. She'd been right. Everything remained as it had been while Bette was alive. Her daughter hadn't cleaned the casita out yet. "I was wondering if you might have some spot cleaner I could use. There are a couple of places on my carpeting that I'd like to attend to."

"Don't you bother yourself about that," Shirley said. "You point them out to me the next time I clean your apartment, and I'll take care of it for you."

"Oh, it's no bother." Lilliana tried to figure out a way to explore more of Bette's home. She wouldn't find anything that would tell her about Bette's valuable secret standing in the doorway. Or anything else that might be a clue. She took another step inside. "My, Bette had some beautiful things, didn't she."

She scrutinized an oil painting on the wall behind the couch. It looked like an original DeGrazia.

Shirley followed her gaze. "Yes, she does. Did. I don't particularly care for that one myself, but there's a nice painting in the master bedroom I always fancied."

"Really? Do you think I could see it?"

"I don't see why not. It's not like Mrs. Tesselink is gonna be looking at it any more."

Lilliana followed Shirley through the living room, turning her head back and forth to see if anything in sight hinted at a motive for Bette's murder. Within seconds, she knew it would take more than the casual glances she was able to manage for that.

Opposite the couch, on either side of the television, the wall was covered with photographs, many in black and white, showing Bette and a handsome young man on a cruise, at the Grand Canyon, the Golden Gate Bridge, at the Statue of Liberty and the Capitol, and all the standard tourist sites. More recent photos of family celebrations showed a Christmas tree in the background or the Thanksgiving turkey on a dining room table surrounded by smiling faces.

Lilliana recognized Susan in several of them, along with a man Lilliana had never seen, but whom she assumed to be Susan's husband, and two adorable little girls. Hmmm. Lilliana hadn't known Bette had grandchildren. Unlike most of the residents, who would chew your ear off with tales of the latest achievements of their grandchildren, whipping out pictures at every opportunity, she couldn't remember Bette ever talking about hers. Odd.

Shirley turned into the master bedroom and stopped just far enough inside the doorway for Lilliana to enter. Her finger pointed at a huge painting over the bed. "Now that is a picture!"

She could see why Shirley preferred this painting to the one in the living room. A large red mountain lighted by the rising sun filled the upper half of the picture. Below, still in shadow, a saguaro cactus and desert brush flanked a trail leading off into the desert. The landscape was realistic, while the DeGrazia was more whimsical, more primitive. Lilliana had been to the DeGrazia Gallery often when she lived in Tucson. She wasn't an art expert, but she estimated the DeGrazia was worth at least ten times what the landscape was. "Very pretty."

While Shirley admired the painting, Lilliana cast furtive glances around the room, searching for anything unusual. It was impossible. Without having some idea of what she was looking for, there was no way to determine where it might be. A fur coat? That would be in the closet. The deed to a silver mine? That might be in a dresser drawer or a desk or stuck in back of a drawer in the kitchen. Lilliana sighed, drawing

Shirley's attention away from the painting.

"Well, I need to get back to work, Ms. Wentworth. You remind me about those spots next time." Shirley turned, and Lilliana proceeded out the bedroom door ahead of her, still keeping her eyes open.

A beautiful silver collection was displayed on the oak sideboard in the dining room, a set of dishes behind the glass doors of the matching china cabinet. Silver candlesticks sparkled on the dining room table. Bette didn't own a desk or a computer as best as Lilliana could tell. It seemed to Lilliana that she remembered talking to Bette once about email, and Bette saying she didn't get along with machines.

"Thank you, Shirley. I'll leave a note on the refrigerator for you if I don't expect to be home the next time you clean my apartment."

"That'll be fine. I'll take care of it." Shirley had already gone back to her dusting before Lilliana left the casita.

* * *

She closed the door to her apartment behind her. It was still too early for Lenny to be home. Although she couldn't water without the fertilizer, she could spend some time grooming her plants. Perhaps she would propagate some leaves as well, get some new plants started to replace the ones she'd sold. With over fifty African violets, there was always something to tend to.

She started in the bathroom, not only because those were her special plants, but because she kept her supplies in an over-the-tank cabinet. Where most people stored bandages and shampoo and bottles of aspirin, Lilliana kept brushes and small knives and a magnifying glass and fertilizer and pesticides. She touched her hand to the door of the second bedroom as she passed, an unconscious action, then opened the door to the bathroom on the opposite side of the hall. As always, a smile touched her lips at the sight.

She slid open the door to the cabinet over the toilet, took out the small scissors, and picked up the first plant. She turned it around in her hand, looking for blossoms past their prime and leaves with any signs of decay. Carefully she removed the spent blossoms and damaged leaves, dropping them in the waste basket. When she was satisfied, she put down the first plant and picked up the next, repeating the process. Later on, she'd sterilize the scissors and cut off fresh leaves for rooting, putting them in plastic bags labeled by variety.

Time passed quickly as she did what she loved best. Being closeted with her African violets immersed her in her own private garden, a foreign land very different from the desert outside. She finished the last plant and stretched out the tightness in her shoulders. She had to remember not to work hunched over for such long periods of time.

She didn't know what time it was, but she imagined Lenny would be back from his trip to town with Nancy. She should see if she could talk to him now. She washed her hands, dried them, and picked up the waste basket to empty it. It wouldn't do to leave rotting vegetation in her plant room acting as an incubator for who knows what molds and fungi and pests.

When she dumped the detritus in her kitchen garbage pail, she spied her cell phone charging on the kitchen counter. Usually she carried it with her, but she had been so eager to look for the spring this morning, she'd forgotten to take it. She unplugged the phone and noticed she had a voicemail message.

Who would have called her? There was only one way to find out.

"Good morning, Lilliana. This is Ted. I was wondering if you'd like to have lunch again today and help me with this plant I bought. It seems to be drooping already."

Lilliana glanced at the clock. Eleven-thirty. She had barely enough time to clean up a little and walk into town. Her fingers trembled like a teenager's as she punched the option to call Ted back.

CHAPTER FOURTEEN

Lilliana picked up her pace as she hurried down the driveway toward the town of Rainbow Ranch. She certainly was getting her exercise today. And just this morning she'd been thinking she might need to join the water aerobics class.

She stopped to catch her breath once she reached Pulaski's Gourmet Grocery. She didn't want to be gasping for air when she talked to Ted, who was waiting on a customer when she opened the door. When the customer turned around, Lilliana was surprised to see Kirstie. Wasn't Kirstie supposed to be on duty now?

Kirstie blanched when she spotted Lilliana, and she clasped a paper bag to her stomach as if protecting it. "Why, hello, Mrs. Wentworth."

"Hello, Kirstie. Have some shopping to do?"

"Oh. Oh, yes." Kirstie held up the bag now, as if to show it wasn't anything unusual. "I ran out of a few things in the clinic and decided it was better to come here rather than wait for our normal delivery."

Odd, thought Lilliana. She would have thought Kirstie would more likely find clinic supplies at the drug store than the grocery.

"Well, I better get back. Someone might be waiting for me." With that, Kirstie rushed toward the door and rapidly exited.

"I'm so glad you could make it for lunch today," Ted said as he came out from behind the counter. "I knew I'd have trouble with that plant."

He went through his ritual of turning the sign on the door to closed, holding the door for Lilliana, then locking it behind him. "Would you like to go to the café for lunch again?"

"Is there anywhere else?" Lilliana asked.

"Well, as a matter of fact, there is." Ted's face reddened. "I was thinking we might go to my house to eat. That way you could see my African violet and show me what I'm doing wrong."

Lilliana was somewhat taken aback. Raised in an era and a society that didn't approve of ladies going to gentlemen's houses alone, the idea of going to Ted's both worried and titillated her. Would he try something? Did she want him to? Don't be silly, she told herself. You'll be perfectly safe. And, if the food was inedible—Lilliana having experienced what bachelors considered food before—she could easily wait until dinner to eat if necessary. "Why, that would be nice."

Ted smiled in relief. "Good. This way."

He turned right, crossed Canyon Road and headed south. After a short distance, he turned onto a little side street called Calle del Sol—Street of the Sun. The street was lined with small territorial houses on large lots. The territorials were constructed of adobe, with flat roofs and vigas, wooden roof beams, protruding along the tops of the walls. The neat yards, mostly weed-free, planted with assorted cacti and agaves, showed pride of ownership, but didn't have the manicured look of being professionally landscaped. Ted turned in at the third house and led the way to the front door.

The house was cool inside. That was one of the benefits of the old, thick adobe walls. They kept out the heat of the Arizona sun. A beehive fireplace in the far corner, which wasn't all that far away, was the focal point of the living room. The house sported a lived-in look, the furniture slightly worn, the rugs on the tile floor slightly faded, a layer of dust covering the tables. An archway at the back of the room led to other parts of the house.

"It's very nice," Lilliana said. "Have you lived here long?"

"I bought the house when I sold the ranch," Ted said. "About ten years ago."

"That long? I thought you gave up your property more recently." The retirement home had only been open three or four years.

Ted nodded. "Yes, that long. Of course, it doesn't seem long compared to the time I lived on the ranch."

"But what was Ellison doing for all those years before he opened the retirement home?"

"Getting permits. Zoning changes. All the usual bureaucratic stuff. A lot of people in Rainbow Ranch feared the town would become too populated, too citified, if they allowed him to build. He eventually convinced them of the benefits to their businesses. And, when people expressed concerns about an increase in crime, he volunteered to finance the police department. We didn't have one before. We let the county sheriff take care of what we needed, which wasn't much."

"It's not a very big police department," Lilliana commented.

Ted smiled. "Well, no. Ellison bought the police car and started a fund with enough to pay a year's salary for the chief. It's not as if we ever had a crime wave to deal with. Until now."

"I wouldn't exactly call this a crime wave," Lilliana said. "So far, all we have is one murder."

"True. But that's one more than we've had in my lifetime. Would you like to eat first or look at the plant?"

"Where is the African violet?" Lilliana started looking for the S. Ionantha and spied it just as Ted gave her the answer.

"Right there." He pointed at a table in front of a window next to the door.

The African violet did look sad. In only a couple of days, several of the flowers had turned brown around the edges, and the leaves were wilting. Lilliana stuck a finger in the soil. It was bone dry. She examined the light coming in the window with a critical eye.

"There are two things African violets need," she said. "Water and sunlight." When she saw the blank look on Ted's face, she quickly added, "I know. Every plant needs those. But African violets, if they're to bloom and thrive, are particular about both."

Ted was paying close attention. He apparently cared about the plant and wanted to improve his knowledge, so Lilliana went on. "Did you see how I stuck my finger in the soil?"

Ted nodded.

"It should feel damp, but not wet to the touch. The soil is too dry. This is a self-watering pot, so you only need to fill the bottom part and let the water percolate up through the soil to the roots.

"The light looks okay, but you may need to adjust that as time goes on. Direct sunlight is often too strong in Arizona. You might have to pull the curtains closed later in the year."

"But why are the flowers dying?" Ted asked.

"That could be totally normal. Species plants don't hang on to their blossoms very long. Or it could be shock at a change in the environment. Don't be afraid to pull them off. You don't want all the water and nutrients to go to dying blossoms. You want those used to grow new blossoms."

Lilliana paused and considered. "The air is rather dry here." Her sinuses were already complaining about the lack of moisture. She'd gotten so used to the humidity in her apartment, she didn't think about how dry other people's homes were. "It will probably take time for this little fellow to adjust. You might need to increase the humidity around the plant."

"How do I do that?"

"Well, start with putting a pebble tray underneath the pot." When Ted looked puzzled, Lilliana described what a pebble tray was. "You can use any watertight tray, about an inch high. Fill it with clean stones or marbles, then add water. The stones give the water more surface area from which to evaporate. You also might want to make a mini-greenhouse by tenting some plastic sheeting over the pebble tray. That will keep the water vapor inside."

Ted pressed his lips together. He looked overwhelmed by the amount of information. "Will I have to do that all the time?"

"No. You can gradually open up the tent and let more of the dry air in. You mostly need it while the violet gets over the shock of moving from my apartment."

"This is a lot more complicated than I expected." Ted's expression told her he was not convinced he could grow an African violet.

"Oh, you'll get used to it." Lilliana laughed.

"I hope so." Ted turned away from the window and asked, "Are you ready for lunch now?"

"Certainly."

Ted led the way through the arch at the back of the room into a sunny kitchen. A table on one side of the room, painted in turquoise and topped with tile in bright Mexican designs, could easily seat six people. Ted opened the refrigerator and took out a Tupperware container and a large, green bowl and put them on the table. Then he opened a cabinet and removed two plates, got flatware out of a drawer, and took a package of Kaiser rolls out of an old-fashioned bread box. Lilliana hadn't seen one of those since she was a child.

"The food may not be fancy, but it's good." Ted sat at the table and removed the covers from the bowl and the Tupperware.

If Lilliana wasn't mistaken, the bowl contained potato salad. The Tupperware container held slices of roast beef, ham, and American cheese. She picked up the serving spoon and scooped some potato salad onto her plate.

Ted put slices of ham on a roll, squeezed mustard on top, then added a slice of cheese.

Lilliana did the same and then commented, "I see you shop at that Pulaski Gourmet Grocery in town."

Ted quickly covered his mouth to keep from spitting out food as he laughed. "They carry good cold cuts." He took a sip of iced tea. "I made the potato salad myself. I'd like to sell homemade potato salad in the store, but preparing it takes too much time to keep it in stock."

She tasted the potato salad. It was quite good. "Do I taste dill?"

"You have a discerning palate. Yes, I use dill and paprika and a dash of dried mustard."

There was silence as they ate their food. After a few more bites, Lilliana said, "I found that spring you told me about."

The hand holding Ted's ham and cheese sandwich stopped halfway to his mouth. "You did?" He seemed to be waiting, almost as if he were hoping she'd deny her last statement.

"Yes, I did. The first pond is a bit muddy, but the stream itself is quite clear and refreshing."

"First pond?" Ted's right eyelid twitched.

Lilliana nodded. "Yes, the first pond. You must know there's a second one farther up the side of the mountain."

"Yes, I've been there. I'm just surprised you went that far." Ted forced his hand to bring his sandwich to his mouth and took a small bite.

"Oh, it's not all that far. I would have gone farther if I hadn't run into a herd of javelinas."

Ted started chewing his sandwich slowly. After he swallowed, he said, "I didn't know there was a herd back there."

Lilliana recounted her adventure with the javelinas and the tree, trying to turn it into a funny story even though she had been terrified at the time. "I might go back to the pond another day."

Ted's head jerked up. "You will?" He recovered and added,

"What about the javelinas?"

"Oh, I doubt that they'll harm me. I just startled them today. Now that I know they come to the upper pond to drink, I'll watch out for them. I'm sure I'll be okay."

"Maybe I should come with you," Ted said.

"That's really not necessary, Ted," Lilliana said. "Besides, you have a store to run."

Ted glanced up at a clock on the wall. "Yes, I do. And I'd better get back so I can open it. Do you want any more potato salad? Would you like some to go?"

Tasty as it was, Lilliana doubted she'd eat any more today. She declined, saying something about having some another time. She wasn't just being polite, as she had been with Nancy. She meant it and hoped to enjoy more of the potato salad in the future. Along with Ted's company.

CHAPTER FIFTEEN

As Lilliana crossed Main Street on her way back to the retirement community, she thought over her lunch with Ted. It had been pleasant, but not at all as warm as the first one. Ted's behavior had been strained, particularly after she told him about finding the stream. It struck her as odd, since he'd been the one to tell her about it in the first place.

All the energy triggered by the joy of anticipation at seeing Ted again drained out of her body. Her usually firm muscles felt like banana cream pudding, barely capable of pushing one foot in front of the other. What she had interpreted as a personal interest when they'd first lunched together had been wishful thinking.

Get hold of yourself, Lilliana. You were lucky enough to be part of one wonderful relationship. That should be enough for a lifetime. She shook off her malaise, straightened her posture, and focused on the day ahead.

As she strode up the driveway, her thoughts turned to her unaccomplished errand. In her excitement, she'd forgotten about her appointment with Lenny. She hoped the heat of the day had kept him off the tennis court and delayed his fishing trip with Nancy until it was cooler. She planned to visit him, borrow the plant food, and ask some probing questions. Lilliana quickened her pace.

A few minutes later, she rapped on the door of Lenny's apartment.

He opened the door a couple of inches, a frown on his face. His puzzled look changed to a warm smile when he saw her standing there. "Lily! Come right in!" Lenny flung the door open and stepped back to allow her to pass.

Nancy wasn't anywhere in sight, which eased Lilliana's mind. She wanted to talk to Lenny alone.

Lilliana stepped inside and took in the interior of the apartment. It dawned on her that, until today, she'd rarely been inside any other resident's apartment. Nor had anyone been in hers. She hadn't noticed the lack until it was no longer true.

While not overly gregarious, Lilliana hadn't been such a hermit for most of her life. She'd had the usual share of friends and acquaintances. But when she and Charles came to Rainbow Ranch after his stroke, she stuck close to him until he passed. She hadn't been interested in talking to other people, hadn't joined in activities like the African Violet Club, until recently. Although it felt traitorous to think so, perhaps a year of mourning was enough.

"What a lovely place," she said. To the right, a small walnut dinette set stood in front of a doorway that led to the kitchen. Most of the living room was taken up by furniture. A sofa, love seat, and chair in a green tweed fabric clustered around a coffee table. Not surprisingly, there were shelves filled with African violets near the sliding glass door that led to the patio. Another plant shelf, closer to the dining area, flanked the television opposite the couch.

"It's not much, but it's home." Lenny closed the door behind her. "You're here for the fertilizer, right?"

Lilliana nodded. "If it's not too much bother."

"No bother at all. Let me step into the kitchen a moment and get it for you." Lenny entered the doorway behind the dinette set, and Lilliana followed. Lenny's kitchen was about the same size as hers, which was to say not very big at all. The stove and refrigerator were to the right, a double sink and dishwasher to the left.

The kitchens at Rainbow Ranch weren't really meant for cooking. Management assumed you'd eat most of your meals in the dining room, so there wasn't much storage. A few cabinets hung on one wall, and one of those fancy juicers sat on the counter. Chunks of cucumber, apple, and a partially peeled lemon lay on a cutting board beside the juicer.

Lenny opened one of the cabinet doors and pulled out a small plastic container, then bent down and took a box from the cabinet under the sink.

While Lenny poured fertilizer from the box into the container, Lilliana continued her perusal of the kitchen. She noticed an assortment of prescription bottles not quite as large as what Kirstie had taken out of Bette's apartment. Once again, she thanked God that she was healthy enough that she didn't have to take a lot of medications.

She didn't mean to be nosy, but her eyes were drawn to the labels. Lipitor, atenolol, Prilosec, Celebrex. All brands she'd seen advertised in the magazines for old people at the doctor's office. One box in particular was striking, white with a series of blue stripes along the bottom and Striant printed in large blue letters. She'd never heard of that one. Of course, they were always coming up with new drug names. Since she didn't take any, she didn't keep up with them.

After filling the tiny tub, Lenny returned the package of fertilizer to the cabinet and shut the door. "Here you go," he said as he held out the plastic container to Lilliana.

"Thank you."

Lenny picked up a paring knife and resumed peeling the lemon. "I was just about to make my afternoon juice snack. Lots of vitamins, minerals, and antioxidants in it. My own special recipe. Can I offer you a glass?"

Lilliana was about to decline, but then thought this might be her opportunity to question Lenny on what he knew about Bette's murder. And she was curious about that fancy juicer. "That would be lovely, thank you."

"Would you grab the carton of blueberries from the refrigerator for me?" he asked.

Opening the refrigerator in search of the berries, she saw what looked like a fat purple pen lying on the top shelf. Was Lenny getting absent-minded? She reached for it, then read the word Genotropin printed on the side and realized the "pen" was yet another medication. Medicine in the refrigerator, medicine in the kitchen cabinet. She wondered if there were more drugs in the medicine chest in the bathroom.

She found the blueberries and handed them to Lenny.

"Why don't you have a seat while I make the juice." He tossed the cucumber chunks in the hopper and turned the machine on.

Much as she would have liked to observe the process, the loud noise of the machine drove her back to the dining area. Lilliana sat at the small table to wait. The clatter started and stopped several times. After one last whoosh, Lenny appeared in the doorway with two glasses. He placed one in front of Lilliana before sitting down with the other one. The liquid inside filled the glass with a beautiful deep red color.

"Did you give your statement to Chief Cartwright yet?" she asked.

"Not yet," Lenny said. "I don't know what I can tell him that he doesn't already know."

"That's not the point. He needs what we know in writing for his reports. He was disappointed I didn't have anything new for him in mine, but there's nothing I can do about that." She tapped her finger on her glass. "Are you sure you didn't see or hear anything that might be a clue as to who killed Bette?"

Lenny shook his head.

She took a small sip of the juice. She rolled it over her tongue, enjoying the sweetness. She was glad Lenny hadn't made her a drink with kale. She couldn't understand how a bitter leafy vegetable had become all the rage.

"How is the juice?" Lenny asked. "I only use organic fruits and vegetables to make my juices."

"Quite good," Lilliana said, "but isn't it terribly expensive?"

Lenny took a sip from his own glass and savored it in his mouth before swallowing. He closed his eyes and breathed in deeply. His breath came out in a hum of pleasure. After opening his eyes, he smiled at Lilliana and said, "There are some things you just have to indulge yourself with. Mine is organic food." He got a mischievous twinkle in his eye. "I seem to remember someone who buys quite a bit of chocolate at the gourmet grocery. And I'm not talking Hershey's."

"Well, as you say, we all have to indulge in something." Lilliana was surprised Lenny had noticed her buying the chocolate and tried to remember when that could have happened. Usually, she had a small piece of chocolate in the evening with her tea, in her apartment, alone. She couldn't recall Lenny ever being in the grocery when she'd bought it. Ah, well. With so many idle hours to fill, gossip must take up quite a few of them. She supposed there were few secrets kept in Rainbow Ranch.

"Have you decided what you're going to raise for the fall show?" Lenny asked.

Lilliana shook her head. "I'm not sure we'll do a fall sale. This one was so expensive and took so much time to organize."

Lenny raised his eyebrows. "Don't most of us have too much time?"

He had a point. On the other hand, Lilliana was looking forward to not having the show tasks to work on. In addition to reading Shakespeare, she wanted to try a new mystery author. She also wanted to visit the sewing and craft store, perhaps start a crewel embroidery project again. Or join the church choir. She missed singing.

Despite all those idle hours, she'd been the one to do most of the work for the African violet show. "Well, yes, but not too many people wanted to help with the planning. Besides, with so few members, it hardly warrants two events in a year."

"There must be more people who would like to join the club," Lenny said. "We should look for some way to encourage them."

"Frank has an idea about that," Lilliana said. She proceeded to tell Lenny about Frank's plan for the flyers.

"It sounds like a good start. When's our next meeting?"

"Thursday. We decided to have one shortly after the show to discuss the results." Lilliana raised her cup to her lips and drank the last of her juice. "Well, I'd better take this plant food back and water my African violets."

"And I should start working on that statement." Lenny sighed and his face took on a hang-dog expression. "I'm not very good at writing. Never was. I can tell you something, but my brain clogs up when I pick up a pen."

Lilliana saw another opportunity to learn more about what Lenny knew. "You know, I could help you with that."

Lenny's face brightened. "You could?"

"Surely. You could talk to me, and I could take notes and type it up on my computer."

"That would be great, Lily. When can we start?"

Lilliana was tempted to say right now, but there were plants to water now that she had fertilizer. "How about we meet in the library after dinner?"

"Sounds good to me." A broad smile spread over his face. "You're a lifesaver, Lily."

* * *

Lilliana had seen the label on the box Lenny had taken the fertilizer from. He used a cheap brand from one of those big box stores, not the better quality fertilizer most of the African Violet Club members used. She decided to visit Frank and see if he could spare some fertilizer. After a quick visit to her apartment to drop off the container Lenny had filled, she crossed through the lobby to the north wing of the building, where Frank lived.

Lilliana knocked on the door and waited. No one answered. She knocked again, a little louder. She was debating knocking a third time when Frank, wearing a grocer's apron that covered the entire front of his body, opened the door. Smudges of dirt stood out against the pristine white of the apron fabric.

His mouth fell open before he spoke. "Lilliana," he said, quickly recovering. "What can I do for you?"

"I was wondering if I might borrow some fertilizer. I've run out and won't be able to get more until the club order arrives next week."

"Why, of course. Come in." He backed away from the doorway.

Frank's apartment appeared to be a mirror image of Lenny's. Most of his living room was taken up by a chocolate-colored leather sofa and a big screen television on the opposite wall. Two industrial-style end tables on either end of the sofa held blocky brown lamps with square white shades. Definitely a man's home.

"Follow me," Frank said in a mock command. He led the way to the bedroom.

Lilliana gasped when he opened the door. The room was filled with shelves of African violets. Brightly lit from all the plant lights, and with a large humidifier humming in the corner, it was like stepping into a jungle. A riot of color surrounded her, and a slightly musty odor from the damp soil hung in the air. A workbench sat in the center of the room, a stack of newspaper on one side and an assortment of tools on the other.

"What do you think of my plant room?" Frank asked.

"No wonder you grow prize winners. This is absolutely marvelous." Then Lilliana had a thought and glanced over her shoulder to verify that the bathroom was across the hall—the door was slightly ajar and she could see the vanity sink—and that there were no other bedrooms in Frank's apartment. "But where do you sleep?"

"Who needs sleep?" Frank joked. "Well, I guess I do. Did you notice the leather sofa in the living room?"

Lilliana nodded, beginning to figure it out.

"It's a sofa bed. I close it up during the day. I can't afford a two bedroom apartment like some of you richer folks, but raising African violets is my life. My beauties need a bedroom more than I do."

"Well, this is certainly impressive." Lilliana thought back to her puny plant shelves and the tiny bathroom she'd let her plants claim. But she had a second bathroom.

"Let me get that fertilizer for you." Frank turned and opened up a large metal cabinet just behind the bedroom door. Plant supplies filled the interior, and buckets of soil mix sat on the bottom of it. He took a container from a shelf at eye level and went to the workbench. After filling a plastic sandwich bag, he returned the package of fertilizer to the cabinet and shut the door. "Here you go," he said as he held out the bag toward Lilliana.

"Thank you." She reluctantly followed Frank out. She would have liked to have spent more time enjoying the plants.

"Can I offer you a cup of coffee?"

Much as Lilliana hated to decline the offer—she would have loved to discuss Frank's growing techniques with him over a cup of coffee, Lenny's healthy juice was still sloshing around in her stomach. "Perhaps another time. I'll let you get back to your repotting."

"Just let me know when."

CHAPTER SIXTEEN

Lilliana scrutinized Lenny as he entered the library, examining his physique with new eyes.

"Good evening, Lily. Missed you at dinner." Lenny took a chair on the opposite side of the table.

"Oh, I decided to eat early for a change." In reality, she'd met up with Willie for an update on their investigation. Willie hadn't been able to get Ellison to talk to him any further. In fact, Ellison seemed to be avoiding the former police officer.

"You must have been hungry. You weren't at lunch either, and I'm sure the juice wasn't nearly enough." His demeanor was wary, as if he were waiting for her to explain herself.

Her hand strayed to the loose skin under her chin, pinched it between her fingers as she fretted over what he meant. Could he have noticed her interest in his medications? There was really no need for her to explain her actions, and she pretended not to be aware of his unspoken questions. She picked up the pen on top of the yellow legal pad in front of her. "Let's get started, shall we?"

"I'm not sure what to say. It's not like *I* know anything." He emphasized the I a little too strongly. Lenny crooked his arm and scratched the top of his bald head.

Had his biceps always bulged that much?

Always curious, Lilliana had used the Internet to look up the unfamiliar medications she'd seen in Lenny's apartment. It appeared there was an explanation for his unusual bodybuilder physique. Unusual for someone in his seventies that is. And it had little to do with his time on the tennis court or in the exercise room.

It turned out the box of pills labeled Striant was a drug for low testosterone. The purple pen contained human growth hormone. Lilliana might not be an expert on drugs, but she had certainly heard of all the scandals in baseball over performance enhancing drugs, or PEDs. She wondered where he'd gotten them. Certainly not from the clinic, where neither Kirstie nor the doctor who came in once a month for routine physicals on the residents would have prescribed them.

"Let's start from the beginning, then." Lilliana said. "You were at the show before I arrived. Did Bette come in before or after you?"

Lenny scrunched up his face and looked off into the distance. "After, I think." He focused on Lilliana and added, "She was on the opposite side of the room, next to Sarah Higgins, if you remember. I was much more interested in setting up my display than watching who was and wasn't there."

Lilliana had forgotten all about Sarah, a quiet eighty-year-old who lived on the second floor of the south wing. Since Lilliana's apartment was on the first floor, their paths didn't often cross. She made a note to follow up with Sarah as well.

And Pieter Joncker, who won third place in the original hybrid category. Pieter, a husky man in his late sixties, with a graying mustache that curled around his upper lip, was another member of the African Violet Club she didn't know very well. She wondered if Bette attempted to steal Pieter's hybrid as well as hers and Frank's.

"Did you notice Bette talking to anyone in particular before the show began?"

Lenny shook his head. "I think most people tried to avoid talking to Bette. I know I did."

"Oh?" This sounded promising.

His expression went from casual to worried. He rubbed the back of his neck, then leaned forward and lowered his voice. "Listen, this has to be off the record, if you know what I mean." He paused and waited for a response.

Lilliana nodded and put down the pen to show she wasn't going to write anything down. She'd have to trust her not-so-reliable memory and determined to focus on every word Lenny said.

"We all know Bette was irritating."

Lilliana had no argument with that statement.

"She was also mean." He scratched his ear, then took a deep breath. "She found out something about me, something that was none of her business, but could get me in trouble with Ellison."

Lilliana had a good idea what that "something" might be. The retirement home frowned on unauthorized drugs. You had to keep them informed of all your prescriptions and even what vitamins you took. It was a good bet Lenny hadn't told them about the PEDs.

"Anyway, she was blackmailing me. She kept threatening to tell Ellison unless I paid her off. Like I told you this afternoon, I don't have a lot of money. At first she was content with twenty dollars a month. I could squeeze that out of my budget. But lately she'd been hinting it would take more for her to keep her mouth shut. Like twenty dollars a week." He shook his head. "I couldn't possibly afford that."

"Didn't it strike you as odd that she was asking for money?" Lilliana asked. "After all, her late husband was quite successful." She remembered the DeGrazia painting she'd seen in Bette's apartment.

Lenny shrugged. "I don't think I ever thought about it. I was too worried about her telling Ellison and coming up with the money to keep her quiet."

Lilliana wondered if Bette had been blackmailing anyone else. First Frank, now Lenny. Blackmail certainly qualified as a motive. Too bad she'd promised to keep it off the record. They should get back to the official statement. She picked up the pen and poised it over the legal pad. "All right. If Bette didn't talk to anyone inside the dining room, did she leave it at any time?"

"She might have. I seem to remember looking over at her table and noticing she wasn't behind it at one point, but we all left for a few minutes at various times during the show." He stared pointedly at her. "If you remember, I watched your table for you while you ate lunch."

A fist squeezed her gut. Was he insinuating that she'd used that time to murder Bette? She'd thought he was her friend.

Lilliana continued to prompt Lenny with questions, but it appeared he didn't know anything more than the rest of them did. For the record, she wrote down his account of her conversation with Frank and the subsequent argument, but she doubted Chief Cartwright would find anything new in that.

CHAPTER SEVENTEEN

Lilliana hurried along the path toward the casitas. Instead of her usual morning walk, she wanted to attempt another try at getting inside Bette's unit before most people were up and about, and before Frank arrived for his morning cigarette. She knew she stood a better chance of sneaking in through the back at this time of day than later, when the pool area would be filled with sun worshippers and water aerobics classes.

However, she halted once she rounded the pool and came in sight of Bette's casita. The front door stood open.

Several cardboard boxes were stacked on the walk in front of the entrance, the DeGrazia leaning up against them. Definitely not the respect an expensive painting deserved. As she stood inventorying the pile of possessions, a woman approaching middle age came out of the casita with another box.

"Something I can help you with?" the woman asked after she put the box she'd been carrying beside the others.

"You must be Susan," Lilliana said, recognizing her from the pictures she'd seen yesterday.

The woman nodded, then brushed a length of brunette hair back from a face covered in a fine sheen of sweat. The strand wouldn't stay put and fell back in front of her eyes which, Lilliana noticed, were also brown. The woman blew at the hair, which begrudgingly moved just far enough so her eyes could meet Lilliana's.

"I am." She rubbed her hands on the front of her jeans, then extended her right one toward the former librarian. "And you are?"

"Lilliana Wentworth." Lilliana took her hand and gripped it firmly. Susan's hand rested limply in hers, as if she had no enthusiasm for this encounter. "Your mother and I were in the African Violet Club together."

A crease appeared between Susan's eyes, then relaxed. "I seem to remember her talking about you."

Lilliana wondered what Bette had said, since they hadn't known one another very well. Nothing good, she was sure. "I'm so sorry for your loss. Is there anything I can help you with?"

Susan looked Lilliana up and down, as if appraising the older woman's ability to carry things. "Well, I haven't packed up the kitchen yet. If you wouldn't mind emptying the cabinets..."

Surprised that getting inside was going to be so easy, she quickly responded, "Not at all."

The woman turned toward the apartment, and Lilliana hurried after her. As they went inside, Susan said, "My husband will be along with a truck shortly." She turned so they were facing one another. "You know where the kitchen is?"

"Yes, of course." Lilliana headed for the kitchen as if she'd been there a thousand times before rather than only the one time yesterday.

Instead of going back to her packing, Susan hung in the kitchen doorway. "We both had to take the day off from work."

Lilliana looked up from the counter where she'd already started wrapping dishes in newspaper. "Excuse me?"

"Both my husband, Jack, and I had to take the day off from work. Mr. Ellison called and said if we didn't move my mother's things out of here by the end of the week, he was going to have them hauled to the dump."

"That's terrible." She wasn't saying that merely to be polite. Lilliana was genuinely shocked. "You would think he would have some compassion, give you some extra time. It's not as if this place has a waiting list or anything."

Surprise crossed Susan's face before she hung her head and stared at the floor. She mumbled a few words, and Lilliana strained to make them out. "Well, to be honest, mom was behind on the rent. Ellison had been threatening to evict her for the last couple of months."

Now it was Lilliana's turn to be surprised. "I was under the impression that your father had left Bette quite well off."

Susan frowned. "He did. But my mother was not a good custodian of the funds. She bought stuff like that stupid painting. And then there were all those trips she went on. New York, London, even Paris. And those trips to Las Vegas with Mr. Rothenberg."

Bette? Taking trips to Las Vegas with Lenny?

"Oh? I didn't know she and Mr. Rothenberg were close." And Lenny hadn't thought to mention the relationship yesterday. She couldn't remember any trips to Las Vegas—or anywhere—that Bette had taken since she'd known her. Had she forgotten?

No. She was sure about that. If Bette had traveled over the past year, Lilliana hadn't been aware of it. She certainly hadn't heard that Bette had gone away with Lenny. *What other secrets had Bette and Lenny shared?*

Susan looked like she'd bitten into a lemon. "I have no idea what she saw in him. There's something obscene about a man that age looking like that, if you know what I mean."

Lilliana knew exactly what she meant, especially in light of her discovery about how he'd gotten that way.

"Anyway, she liked the slot machines way too much. I told her she had to stop spending her money so extravagantly. There was still enough coming from the annuity to stay here, but she wouldn't listen. She kept taking money out of it to buy more stuff. Which I now have to pack." Susan sighed. "Sorry to dump on you."

"No, no, that's perfectly all right." And useful. Now she understood how Bette had found out enough about Lenny to blackmail him. It just went to show you how you never knew with people.

"Thanks so much for offering to help." Susan smiled.

"It's the least I can do," Lilliana said, hoping she'd also have an opportunity to snoop.

"Well, I'd better get back to it." Susan turned and headed in the direction of the master bedroom.

As soon as Susan was gone, Lilliana stopped packing dishes and started opening drawers. She didn't have any idea what she expected to find in them, but it seemed more likely there would be something of interest in the drawers than in the cabinets. Maybe an address book or a checkbook, a note or a letter.

She found none of those. What she did find was old silverware, potholders, and your typical junk drawer filled with odds and ends: batteries, a flashlight, picture hooks, some coasters. That held more promise. She was about to start pulling the junk out of the drawer and putting it on the counter so she could inspect it, when a deep voice with a Hispanic accent resonated behind her.

"Mrs. Wentworth. I did not expect to find you here."

"Good morning, Miguel." The handyman stood in the doorway, a toolbox in his hand. His chin-length hair looked particularly greasy today, and he hadn't bothered to put a regular shirt on over his tank-style undershirt. The proper librarian in her grimaced.

"Is it okay if I fix the pipe?" Miguel asked.

"The pipe?"

"Under the sink. Mrs. Tesselink reported it was leaking."

Lilliana glanced toward the sink under the window at the end of the kitchen. "I suppose so."

"Gracias." Miguel came in and set his toolbox on the floor near the sink. He opened the cabinet underneath, then got down on the floor and peered inside.

"Is it leaking?" Lilliana asked, trying to make conversation. It seemed to her that it would be worthwhile to talk to anyone who had known Bette Tesselink. You never knew who might have information that would lead to the killer.

Miguel got up and shrugged. "It might be." He turned on the cold water faucet and let it run.

"I've always appreciated the way Rainbow Ranch handles

problems promptly," Lilliana said as Miguel bent down to look under the sink again.

"I wish more people were like you. Mrs. Tesselink"—his face clouded over—"never thought I was fast enough or good enough. Always complaining to the boss about my work."

Lilliana wanted to follow up on that, but just at that moment, Miguel turned on the garbage disposal. It made quite a bit of racket, certainly more noise than the one in her apartment, and she doubted she'd be heard over the sound. Miguel quickly turned the disposal off again. He glanced briefly under the sink. Lilliana craned her neck so she could see as well.

The plop, plop, plop of dripping water reached her ears even as a small puddle formed beneath the pipe.

Miguel looked vindicated. "As I suspected. It is the garbage disposal."

Maybe she should hire Miguel as a detective. "The motor certainly runs very loud."

"She must have put something down it she shouldn't have. People always think they can get rid of all kinds of garbage by putting it down the drain. Then it breaks the unit and I have to replace it. Only she'd never admit to doing anything wrong. She complained the pipe was leaking."

Miguel's voice held so much acrimony Lilliana wondered if he might be a suspect. At this rate, she'd be investigating suspects for the next year.

"I think I have a spare in stock," Miguel said. "I'll get it and be back in a few minutes."

Without saying anything further, Miguel left.

Alone once more, Lilliana began emptying the junk drawer

on the counter, eager to see if it contained any clues. She had just determined there was nothing of interest in it when Miguel returned carrying a new disposal still in its box.

"I see you found the spare," Lilliana said.

"Yes," Miguel said. "I'm glad I didn't have to order one. Mr. Ellison wants to show this casita over the weekend."

"He does?" First Susan said Ellison had pressured her to remove her mother's things from the casita, now Miguel was in a hurry to make repairs to it. As far as Lilliana knew, there were at least two other empty casitas. She couldn't understand the rush to rent this particular one.

Miguel nodded. "It seems so many people came to your plant show, he has several people who want to see the apartments and casitas this weekend."

Lilliana couldn't help but wonder if they were interested in living at Rainbow Ranch—or in seeing the place where the murder victim had lived. She tended to believe it was more the latter than the former.

Miguel opened the box and took out the new disposal, then ducked under the sink and proceeded with his task. Lilliana went back to boxing up dishes.

A short time later, Miguel rose from the floor, the old disposal unit in hand. Lilliana turned at the clanking sound it made as he put it in the stainless steel sink.

"Now let's see what Mrs. Tesselink tried to dispose of," Miguel said. There was more clanking and some grunting, followed by a moment of silence. "Huh."

Lilliana took a few steps toward Miguel so she could see what had come out of the disposal. She drew in a breath so sharply it whistled through her teeth. In the sink, twisted and scarred from the blades of the garbage disposal, sat a little brass key.

"Could I see that?" Lilliana held her hand out to Miguel. He put the key in it. The key wasn't quite as mangled as she'd first thought. While the top of the key skewed at an angle, the blade, the part that actually made the key turn in a lock and move the parts inside, appeared relatively straight. It would probably work to open... whatever. "Do you mind if I keep it?"

Miguel shrugged. "Not at all, señora. I would just throw it in the trash with the garbage disposal." He started packing up his tools.

Lilliana turned the key over in her hand. She doubted Bette had dropped it down the disposal on purpose. More likely, it was an accident, and she had been anxious for Miguel to retrieve the key for her. It wasn't as big as a house key, nor quite as small as one for a metal lockbox or jewelry box. It might fit a small padlock, but there was no brand name on the top part, which Lilliana thought was on all of those. She clearly remembered that the key for the padlock on the gate to the swimming pool fence at her home had had "Master" emblazoned on it.

"Adios, señora," Miguel said as he walked toward the doorway, toolbox in hand. Once he was gone, Lilliana took a careful look around the kitchen. There was nothing here that had a keyhole.

Dropping the key in her pocket, she stepped into the combined living-dining room area and did a quick scan of the room. Nothing in plain sight took a key. Perhaps inside something? She couldn't see anything with a lock on the glassed-in shelves of the china cabinet. She opened the large drawer below, slowly, furtively, being careful not to make any noise that Susan might hear. It contained a silverware chest that did have a lock in it, but the lock was much too small for the brass key. Assorted serving pieces—a couple of crystal candy dishes, a silver condiment dish with glass liners, that kind of thing—took up the rest of the space in the drawer.

Lilliana closed the drawer and proceeded over to the sideboard with a glance down the hall to make sure Susan was still in the bedroom. A brief break in the sound of closet doors and dresser drawers opening and closing worried Lilliana. She didn't want to be discovered snooping around. She waited quietly, holding her breath and trying to come up with a reasonable excuse in case Susan saw her. Lilliana breathed again when the noises from the bedroom resumed.

She opened the left-hand cabinet door and found an assortment of dusty liquor bottles, half of them never opened. Bette hadn't been much of a drinker or, for that matter, hostess. Lilliana opened the cabinet door on the other end of the sideboard and sighed. It was empty.

Opening the drawers in the middle, all she found were table linens. There was a beautiful damask tablecloth with matching napkins as well as several sets more suited to everyday use. Lilliana slid her hands under the piles, careful not to disturb them too much, and felt for anything solid that might use the key. Just as she was about to give up, her fingertips bumped into something hard.

She slid them along the length of it, then down the smooth sides of what felt like a small box. She pulled it to the front of the drawer and folded back the tablecloth, exposing her find.

The box was exquisite. A fountain of delicate flowers and leaves leapt from a Greek urn against the black background of the japanned finish. The enamel felt smooth as silk as she caressed it under her fingers. Measuring approximately ten inches wide and five inches deep, the box couldn't have been more than two inches high. And on the front was a keyhole that appeared to be exactly the right size for the key in her pocket.

Before she could try the key, footsteps thudded from the direction of the open front door. She quickly pushed the box back, covered it with the tablecloth, and closed the drawer before scurrying back to the kitchen. She grabbed another dish and a sheet of newspaper. She hoped her unsteady fingers wouldn't drop the dish as she started to wrap it.

"Hello."

She started at the sound of a strange male voice. Lilliana turned to face a man with the brightest red hair she'd ever seen.

"I thought Susan might be in here," he said. "I'm Jim Frasier, Susan's husband."

She fought to keep her voice light and agreeable, without the nervousness she actually felt. "Pleased to meet you. I'm Lilliana Wentworth. Susan's in the bedroom."

"No, she's not." Susan came up behind Jim. "I heard you come in," she said. "Mrs. Wentworth volunteered to help me pack."

"How nice of her," Jim said. "But I think now that I'm here, we can handle it."

"Right," said Susan. It was clear who was in charge in this family. Susan addressed Lilliana. "Thanks for giving me a hand."

"I was happy to help." She regretfully stopped packing and walked toward the door. The Frasiers moved aside to let her through. Before exiting the casita, she turned and added, "I'll stop by later and see if you need any more help." *And perhaps get a chance to look in that box.*

"Oh, I'm sure we'll be fine. We'll probably be finished before you come back," Jim said.

How odd. As soon as Jim had arrived, he seemed intent on getting rid of her. What didn't he want her to find? Did he know about the box? Did Susan? Or was there something else?

CHAPTER EIGHTEEN

By the time Lilliana got to the dining room, it was almost empty. Glancing at her watch, she noted she'd arrived with five minutes to spare before they stopped serving breakfast. Fortunately, Willie still lingered at a table—alone—so she joined him. Half a plate of food remained in front of him.

"Good morning," Lilliana said as she picked up the day's menu. The waitress appeared at her side immediately, a sour look on her face. Lilliana didn't blame her. She was sure the waitress was looking forward to finishing up her shift and going home. But, for a change, Lilliana's appetite, on a visit from some younger version of herself, hungered for breakfast. She placed her order, and the waitress went to get her food.

"I hoped you'd show up eventually," Willie said.

"Oh?" Lilliana queried. "Did you find out anything?"

Willie looked crestfallen. "No, but I was hoping you had."

Lilliana's food arrived, along with the cup of hot water she'd requested. She took the individually-wrapped package of Earl Grey from her pocket, opened it, and put the teabag in the water to brew. Without pausing, she picked up her fork and cut off a bite of her pancakes. When she finished chewing, she said, "Sorry. I'm very hungry this morning. It's probably all the exercise."

"More than your usual walk?" Willie asked. He picked up his coffee mug and took a sip.

Lilliana nodded and took another bite of her breakfast. Eating definitely interfered with her ability to tell a story, but her stomach cried for food like a newborn baby at three in the morning. "I thought I'd try to get inside Bette's casita and take a look around this morning. When I got there, her daughter, Susan, was already inside packing up. She told me Bette was broke." She paused again and cut up a sausage link and popped a piece in her mouth.

"She was?" Willie's eyes widened, waiting for Lilliana to nod her assent, after which he said, "She didn't act that way."

"No, she didn't," Lilliana agreed.

"In fact, not so long ago she told me she planned on taking another trip to Las Vegas." Willie stared off into space as if remembering.

"Another trip?" The first Lilliana had known about Bette's trips to Las Vegas was when Susan told her about them this morning. She wondered why Willie hadn't thought to mention this detail when they'd first discussed investigating the murder.

"Didn't you know? She and Lenny had been going to Las Vegas every few months for quite some time."

"I never thought of them as a couple. In fact, I don't believe I ever saw them together other than at the African Violet Club meetings. I certainly wouldn't have expected them to travel together." Lilliana puzzled over this information for a moment, then resumed eating her pancakes.

"Well, it's true. For weeks before, Bette was excited about going back, playing the slots, seeing the shows—all the regular stuff people do in Vegas. She usually didn't say much afterwards, though." Willie grinned. "There's a reason it's nicknamed Lost Wages."

Lilliana smiled in return. "You know, Lenny never mentioned the trips either. And it doesn't make any sense in light of what he told me last night."

"Last night?" Willie picked up his coffee cup again. He hadn't touched his food since Lilliana had joined him. Three pancakes swimming in syrup and two sausages cooled on his plate. The remains of an egg smeared a yellow stain across one side. Maybe he was finally trying to take off that weight so he could get his hip replacement.

"Oh, I haven't seen you since then, have I?" Lilliana proceeded to tell him how she'd volunteered to write down Lenny's statement for the police chief. "He claims she was blackmailing him."

"Blackmail sounds like a pretty good motive for murder," Willie said.

"That's what I was thinking." Her plate now clean, Lilliana put down her fork and picked up her teacup. She made a concentrated effort to sip, rather than gulp, the tea. "But I have a hard time imagining Lenny as a killer."

"I would agree, but my experience tells me otherwise."

"What do you mean?"

"You would think it would take something major for one person to kill another. But I've seen kids stab someone to death for a pair of brand name sneakers. Or shoot them for looking at a girlfriend cockeyed."

Lilliana conjured up an ugly picture of teenaged gang members attacking some poor, innocent child for footwear. "But Lenny isn't a teenager. He's a mature man."

"A mature man on a fixed income being squeezed by a blackmailer," Willie said.

"But why wouldn't he go to the police? Or at least report it to Russ Ellison?"

"Did he say why she was blackmailing him?"

Lilliana shook her head. "No, but I have a pretty good idea what it was." She told him about the medications she'd seen in Lenny's apartment.

"And that explains the trips to Las Vegas. At least for him." Willie frowned.

"How?" She didn't understand the connection.

"There's a doctor in Las Vegas, not much younger than Lenny, who prescribes those things for exactly the reasons Lenny is going. You've probably never seen his ads since I doubt you read Sporting News or—uhhh—other magazines."

Lilliana had a good idea what Willie meant by "other" and appreciated his delicacy. But she wasn't exactly a naive young thing.

"He advocates his treatments for staying young and physically vigorous. There's a lot of controversy over it, but no one's shut him down. So far."

"So that explains the alliance. Bette went for the gambling, and Lenny went for the drugs. You never know about people, do you?"

"No, you don't," Willie said. "Are you about ready to leave? I see Peggy is waiting to clear our table."

Lilliana took another look at Willie's half-full plate. "You barely ate anything. Is something wrong?"

Willie glanced down and laughed. "No, no. I'm just not hungry this morning."

Lilliana raised her eyebrows.

"I know, unbelievable, right? Maybe it has something to do with that cookie I found on my nightstand this morning."

"Cookie?" Lilliana thought about the button she'd found on her nightstand.

"Well, more like a wafer, I think. It was quite tasty. Cookie, wafer, it surprised me how quickly it filled me up. I'm still full, and all I ate was an egg and coffee."

"Do you have any idea who left it there?" Lilliana asked.

"Not a clue. I'd like to thank them. And ask where I can buy some more. If I can eat less this easily, I'll get my hip replacement in no time."

"Well, if I hear anything, I'll let you know."

Willie picked up his walking stick from the floor, and the two of them rose from the table and headed out.

* * *

Once she was back in her apartment, Lilliana hurried to her laptop computer and woke it up, impatient at the sluggishness the aging machine exhibited for the first few seconds. Kind of like me, she thought. Only there was no equivalent of a cup of Earl Grey for the computer. She just had to wait until it was ready.

She double-clicked on the membership list for the African Violet Club on her desktop. She had agreed to talk to Sarah Higgins while Willie tried to interview Pieter Joncker. She wasn't sure where Sarah lived, but knew her apartment number would be on the list, as well as a phone number.

It took her a minute to recognize that Mrs. Robert Higgins had to be Sarah. While many of the residents of Rainbow Ranch were single by death, divorce, or never having married, a few couples dwelt at the retirement home as well, most of them in the older age range. She supposed Sarah and—she looked at the list again—Robert fit that category. She thought Sarah was around eighty. Robert was probably a few years older, if they followed the pattern of most couples.

She dialed Sarah's number. "Sarah? This is Lilliana. I wondered if I might come up and speak with you."

Sarah sounded overjoyed at the opportunity. She didn't even ask what about.

The Higginses lived in an upper floor apartment in the same wing as Lilliana. Although there was an elevator in the lobby, Lilliana decided to take the stairs. They were closer, and she could certainly manage one flight of stairs.

By the time she reached the top of them, she almost regretted not taking the elevator. The arthritis in her knees was complaining, and all those muscles she'd used yesterday morning in escaping the javelina reminded her they weren't used to that kind of abuse. Fortunately, Sarah lived in the second apartment from the stairwell on the right-hand side.

"Lilliana! Come in, come in." Sarah waved her into an apartment that was the mirror image of Lilliana's own. Sarah was a tiny woman, under five feet tall, and probably weighed no more than one hundred pounds. She wore her snow white hair in what they used to call a bouffant style, soft curls around her face. You would think the large eyeglasses she wore would overpower her features, but the brightness of her eyes and her constant smile offset the frames.

A television blared one of those old western shows, *Gunsmoke* she thought, in the background. In front of it sat an elderly man built almost as sparely as his wife, except for a little pot belly on which he rested his folded hands. His hairline receded half-way up his scalp, not anything like Lenny's or Willie's bald pates, and the gray hair that remained was somewhat askew, as if he'd been running his hands through it.

"Bob! Bob! Lilliana's here." Sarah announced her arrival as if they were all bosom buddies, even though Lilliana had never met Bob Higgins before.

Bob looked at her and gave a half-hearted wave in her direction.

"Bob! Bob! Put your earphones on so we can talk in peace," Sarah said.

Bob reached down beside the recliner he sat in and picked up a set of headphones from the floor. After he clapped them over his ears, he picked up one of the three remote controls on the table beside him and pressed something that cut off the television sound from the speakers.

"That's better," Sarah said. "Why don't we sit at the dining room table. Can I get you coffee? Tea?"

"Maybe a drink of water," Lilliana said. The climb up the stairs had made her thirsty.

Sarah bustled off into the kitchen. Lilliana sat at the table. In a jiffy, Sarah brought back two large glasses of ice water. "Would you get some coasters from the drawer behind you?"

Lilliana turned and opened the drawer of the buffet, saw the stack of coasters, and picked up two. She put one in front of her place and one in front of the seat next to her for Sarah.

"It's so nice to have company," Sarah said after she sat down. "Bob spends all day watching cowboy shows on that thing." She gestured in the direction of the television. "I have to watch the TV in the bedroom if I want to see my soaps."

Like most members of the African Violet Club, Sarah's perky plants were in evidence, although she only had one lighted shelf just inside the entrance to the apartment.

"Your African violets look like they're doing well," Lilliana commented.

Sarah glanced in the direction of the shelf. "As well as can be expected. I'd love to grow more, but Bob thinks I already make too much of a mess, what with watering and repotting and everything. He's tried to convince me to give up growing them, but I tell him I'll stop growing African violets when he gives up poker night." Her tone of voice permitted no nonsense. Lilliana would hate to argue with this woman.

"Well, not everyone has to be as obsessed with African violets as Frank is. Did you know he's turned his bedroom into a plant room?" Lilliana asked.

"Really? How many plants do you think he has?"

Lilliana did a quick estimate. "Oh, several hundred at least. Maybe a thousand." Until now, she hadn't realized how many plants Frank nurtured in that bedroom. That was incredible!

"It's terrible about what happened to Bette, isn't it?" Sarah said.

Lilliana should have known it wouldn't take much to get Sarah talking about the murder. With so little excitement, she was sure all the Rainbow Ranch residents spent a good part of the day speculating about it. "Yes, it is. As a matter of fact, that's what I wanted to talk to you about."

"Me?" Sarah seemed surprised.

"You," Lilliana affirmed. "You had the display table right next to hers at the show. I was wondering if she said anything to you that might be related to her murder."

Sarah looked thoughtful. "Not that I remember. We didn't talk all that much."

"I can understand that," Lilliana said. "Most people had trouble getting along with her."

"Oh, I didn't have any trouble with Bette. I meant we didn't have time to talk, what with setting up our tables before the show. Then all those people started coming in, and Russ Ellison made his speech and…" Sarah held her hands out to the side, palms up, and shrugged her shoulders.

"Did anyone come over to speak with her?"

Sarah looked confused. "You and Frank, of course."

"No one else?"

Sarah shook her head.

Lilliana tried another question. "Did she leave her table at any time?"

Sarah shook her head again. "I don't remember her leaving."

Although it appeared as if Sarah didn't have anything to add, Lilliana couldn't very well get up and leave right away. It would be terribly impolite. And Sarah seemed so desperate for company, Lilliana didn't have the heart to leave her alone again. "Are you going to be at the next meeting?"

"Next meeting? Oh, of the club. I suppose so."

"I'm glad to hear that. We need all the members we can get, and you, as president, should be there to meet them. Russ Ellison thinks our show was so successful, he'd like us to put on another one in the fall." She watched for Sarah's reaction.

She wanted to get a feel for what the membership felt about this before she put it to a vote at the meeting.

Sarah's reaction was one of alarm. "So soon? I mean, it's so much work." She glanced over at her plant stand. "And I'm not sure I can grow too many more plants in that short a time."

"I wouldn't worry too much about that. I think Frank has enough to sell for all of us." She chuckled and Sarah joined her. Lilliana took a sip of her water.

Sarah looked wistful as she said, "It was fun, though. All the people who came to the show were so nice. And they said such nice things about my plants. Bette's, too. They particularly liked the blue one she won the prize for."

Lilliana bristled at mention of the stolen hybrid but decided not to rehash that with Sarah.

"Except for that one man. He was practically yelling at her. Only not quite as loudly as you were." Sarah looked pointedly at her.

"What one man?" Lilliana perked up. A new lead! She ignored the implied criticism of her behavior.

"You must know him," Sarah said. "The one who runs that expensive convenience store in town. He has a funny name." Sarah furrowed her brow as she tried to come up with it.

"You mean T—Mr. Pulaski?" Lilliana was incredulous. Why would Ted be arguing with Bette Tesselink?

Sarah nodded. "Yes, that's the one."

"Did you hear what were they arguing about?"

"Not really. He just kept saying 'we have to talk,' and she just kept saying 'not now' and shaking her head."

Lilliana was totally flummoxed. This was something she would never have expected. She'd have to talk to Ted and find out what he'd wanted to discuss with Bette. She discretely looked at her watch. It was a little after eleven. Plenty of time to walk into town before lunch.

"Well, it's been nice talking to you, Sarah."

Sarah looked disappointed. "It was nice talking to you, too. We'll have to do this more often."

With a twinge of guilt, Lilliana doubted she'd be visiting Sarah very much in the future. Maybe she could make an effort to be a bit more friendly. "I'll see you at the meeting then."

Sarah brightened. "Yes, of course."

Lilliana made her escape and headed for the elevator. She wanted to avoid more strain on her knees and save her strength for the walk into town.

CHAPTER NINETEEN

She studied Ted's face from across the table. He looked older than she remembered, a wattle at his neck, deep creases in his cheeks and around his bright blue eyes from years spent in the sun and wind as a cowboy. His mustache consisted of mostly gray, as did the hair that curled over his collar. It hadn't been any trouble to get him to agree to lunch again. In fact, he'd been eager to go with her. On another occasion, she would have been as eager to go with him, had her reason not been her suspicions in a murder investigation.

"A penny for your thoughts," he said.

"I'm not sure they're worth that much." Lilliana laughed nervously.

He raised his bushy eyebrows, then lowered them. He picked up a spoon and stirred his coffee. "My African violet seems to be doing better today. I've been trying to do like you told me."

Lilliana nodded. "African violets aren't really that hard to grow. I'm sure you'll do fine with it."

An awkward silence stretched between them. Lilliana

deliberated over how to broach the subject of Ted's discussion with Bette Tesselink. Relief flooded her tightened chest when the waitress arrived bearing plates of food. She busied herself with cutting the burrito on her plate and putting some in her mouth. Ted picked up a piece of fried chicken, a drumstick, and attacked it with his teeth.

She decided to ease into the subject she needed to pursue. "I talked to Sarah Higgins this morning."

Ted squinted in concentration, and Lilliana realized he probably didn't know who Sarah was. She'd started to think of Ted as part of the retirement community, but obviously he wasn't. "Sarah had the table next to Bette's at the show."

The squint around Ted's eyes relaxed. "Older lady, right?"

"That's right," Lilliana said, although Sarah was younger than Ted. She put another piece of burrito in her mouth and tried to swallow past the lump in her throat. It took a sip of iced tea to get the burrito all the way down. She put down her fork. "Sarah said you spoke to Bette on Saturday."

Ted's eyes widened in alarm, then a bland mask dropped over his face. "I spoke to most of the sellers at the show. Asking questions about their plants and trying to decide who I'd buy one from." He smiled engagingly and looked into her eyes. "I'm glad I picked you."

Lilliana averted her gaze. "Sarah seemed to think you were arguing."

"Arguing?" Ted pulled back and blinked his eyes rapidly several times. "I can't imagine why she'd think that."

"She also said you told Bette you wanted to talk to her about something." The closer she got to what she wanted to know, the harder Lilliana's heart thumped in her chest.

Ted finished gnawing the rest of the meat off his drumstick. He took his napkin from his lap and wiped his hands before deliberately picking up his fork. He scooped up some corn. After chewing and swallowing, he said, "Just about African violets. I don't know what else I'd talk about to anyone at the show."

Lilliana thought a moment. Was it possible Sarah had misinterpreted the discussion? Maybe she wanted to tell Lilliana what she thought she wanted to hear, something exciting to liven up her apparently rather commonplace life with Bob. A dead end.

Relieved, Lilliana said, "So how is your fried chicken?"

"Excellent, as always." He picked up a French fry, dipped it in a blob of ketchup on his plate, and stuck it in his mouth.

"So is my burrito. It's too bad this café is so far off the beaten track. I'm sure it would be a great success and draw a lot more business in Bisbee."

Ted playacted an exaggerated glance to the left and right, then leaned over. "Shhh. Don't tell Cathy that. If she moves the café to Bisbee, where will I eat?" He flashed her a grin. "Speaking of Bisbee…"

"Yes?"

Ted stared at his plate as he said, "I'm thinking about taking a trip in next Sunday afternoon. The saloon in Brewery Gulch offers live music then, and I like to go listen. Any chance you'd like to go with me?" He raised his eyes to meet Lilliana's.

She wasn't sure how to respond. He was asking her on a date. She hadn't been on a date in over fifty years. *Well, why not? It might be fun.*

As she was about to accept, Chief Cartwright walked into

the restaurant and headed straight for the booth where Lilliana and Ted sat.

"Lilliana Wentworth, you're under arrest for the murder of Bette Tesselink."

Lilliana's mouth opened in a large "O" at the words spoken by Chief Cartwright. The proverbial jaw-drop. Catching flies. Whatever the cliché, she couldn't believe what she'd heard. She closed her mouth and swallowed. "What do you mean?"

The police chief glanced around the room nervously and cleared his throat. In a voice that almost quivered, he repeated much less firmly, "You're under arrest for the murder of Bette Tesselink." His voice squeaked a little on the last syllable.

"That's ridiculous," Lilliana said. "On what grounds?"

The chief's eyes darted from side to side. Lilliana followed his gaze and realized every eye in the place was focused on the two of them. Chief Cartwright lowered his voice to almost a whisper. "Let's discuss that at the police station." He stared pointedly around the room again.

"Oh, all right," Lilliana said. She put her napkin on the table and rose from her seat. "Sorry about the interruption to our lunch, Ted."

Ted reached out and put his hand on top of hers. "Let me come with you."

Cartwright picked up on this remark and shook his head. "I can only take the prisoner in my patrol car."

Lilliana was about to argue, but they'd already made enough of a scene in the café. "I'll be fine," she told Ted. "It will just take a few minutes to straighten this out."

Ted appeared doubtful, but concurred with her statement— for the moment. "Okay. But let me know if you need me." He scribbled something on a napkin and handed it to Lilliana.

She glanced down at the scrap of paper and saw a phone number. She stuck the piece of paper in her pocket. Her fingertips brushed the key that was still there. She'd totally forgotten to tell Willie about it this morning. Oh, well. It probably wasn't important.

She turned her eyes toward the police chief and was amazed to see him holding a pair of handcuffs.

"Surely you don't think I'm going to attack you in the patrol car or try to make a desperate escape, young man."

"It's procedure. Please hold your hands out in front of you." Young Cartwright looked slightly worried for a minute, as if afraid she wouldn't comply. Then his jaw set and his eyes locked on hers as he extended the handcuffs another fraction of an inch in her direction.

Lilliana sighed and held out her hands. She would argue with him once they got away from the crowd.

After fastening the cuffs, the chief grasped her elbow and guided Lilliana toward the door. She could feel the eyes of the entire clientele of Cathy's Café following them.

It took longer to get in and out of the police car with the handcuffs hindering her movements than it did to drive to Town Hall. Cartwright marched her through the lobby and closed the door to his office once they were inside. After she was seated, she held out her wrists. "Are these really necessary?"

Chief Cartwright regarded her for a minute, then said, "I suppose not." He unlocked the handcuffs and put them back on his duty belt.

Lilliana rubbed her wrists. Even in the short time she'd had them on, they'd left red marks. "Now please tell me what this is all about."

The chief picked up a folder from his desk and opened it. "I received the results of the forensics tests and the ME's report. One," he ticked the number off on the index finger of his right hand, "Bette Tesselink died of blunt trauma to the head consistent with a wound made by a baseball bat."

"Softball bat," Lilliana corrected as he paused to take a breath.

"Softball bat," the chief said, but Lilliana was sure the report had baseball bat written in it. People who didn't play didn't know there was a difference.

The chief raised his middle finger and said, "Two. The bay —softball bat at the scene of the crime contained blood, hair, and tissue matching that of the victim. It also had your fingerprints on it."

"Of course it did," Lilliana said. "It's my bat."

Chief Cartwright nodded. "Correct. Three. You have admitted that the murder weapon belongs to you." Before Lilliana could inject anything else, he hurriedly said, "There was no evidence that anyone—other than the housekeeping staff— had been in the room that day. You have also admitted that you argued with the victim earlier in the day."

"Well, we knew all of that the minute Bette turned up dead."

The chief ignored her comment. "Motive, means, and opportunity. You were angry at her for purportedly stealing your plant, you brought the softball bat with you to the show, and you were alone with the victim in the storage room. The evidence all supports this."

Lilliana frowned and shifted in her chair. For the first time since she'd found Bette's body, she believed she actually might be convicted of murder. But, surely… She realized Chief Cartwright didn't have all the information she and Willie had gathered over the past couple of days. Feeling better, she sat up straight and said, "There are some things you ought to know, Chief."

"I think I know enough." He started to rise.

"But you don't know everything." She cleared her throat. "First of all, I wasn't the only one who had a motive to kill Bette Tesselink. It seems as if she was blackmailing at least two people at the retirement home."

Chief Cartwright's chair cushion whooshed as his weight dropped back onto it. "Who? What for?"

"Well, Frank Bellandini for one. He's been smoking behind Bette's casita, and Bette caught him at it. There's no smoking on the grounds of the retirement home." She thought she should make the reason clear. "Bette threatened to go to Russ Ellison and report Frank if he didn't pay her."

"That's a pretty minor offense," Cartwright said.

"Not at Rainbow Ranch. Most of the residents are sick. We're all old. Russ Ellison prides himself on having a healthy environment for his residents. If he found out Frank was smoking, there's a good chance he'd kick him out and make him forfeit whatever rent was due on the remainder of his lease.

"The other one I know about is Leonard Rothenberg. You must know him, at least by sight, if not by name. He's the one who looks like a bodybuilder."

Cartwright nodded. "I wish I could have his body."

"Well, you could," Lilliana said, "if you took the drugs he

takes. Yes, he exercises and plays a lot of tennis, but that's not all he does. He takes things to keep that body. We're supposed to report all our prescription medications to Kirstie so she has a record of them. I'm sure Lenny never reported those. Bette found out about them on one of their trips to Las Vegas."

The chief looked more interested now. "I've heard about Mrs. Tesselink and how she aggravated people. Most of the statements I got made a point of mentioning that. But why would she blackmail them? The witnesses also talked about how much money she had, how she lived in an expensive casita instead of one of the apartments."

"What they didn't know," Lilliana said with a bit of smugness, "was that Bette was broke. She spent all the money her husband left her, a lot of it on those trips to Las Vegas."

Chief Cartwright steepled his fingers in front of his lips and leaned back in his chair as he digested this information. Suddenly he straightened and lowered his hands. He leaned forward across the desk and pointed a finger in her face. "But you were the one with the bat, and your prints were on it."

"Oh, tosh! Anyone could have used my bat. The door to the storage room wasn't locked. And the killer probably wore gloves. We all know about that from watching television."

"Could have and did are two different things, Mrs. Wentworth. All the evidence points to you as the killer. No matter how many stories you tell me, that hasn't changed. I have a warrant for your arrest." He held up the legal document so she could see it. "And I'm going to take you down to the county jail and book you. I'll let the court figure things out."

Chief Cartwright stood up and took the handcuffs off his belt again. "Hold out your hands."

Lilliana felt like she was in the middle of a nightmare. Hadn't the Chief heard a word she said? If he had, he apparently hadn't believed her. Surely a good lawyer would be able to prove her innocence, but at the moment it appeared as if she was going to be spending some time in a cell.

She didn't even know a lawyer. At least, not a criminal lawyer. There was that one in Tucson who had changed her will after Charles had passed away. She wasn't even sure she remembered his name.

"Mrs. Wentworth?" The chief was waiting.

Resigned, Lilliana held out her hands again. She was going to take a ride to Bisbee whether she wanted to or not. After the cuffs were on, Cartwright opened the office door.

Ted Pulaski stood there, his hand raised and poised to knock.

"Just one minute, Chief."

CHAPTER TWENTY

Chief Cartwright looked as surprised as Lilliana felt at seeing Ted Pulaski. The chief stood, immobile, facing the grocer and former ranch owner, wavering between inviting Ted in and pushing him out of the way.

"Please? Just give me a few minutes." The earnestness of his plea was echoed in the expression on Ted's face. Apparently the combination convinced the chief in favor of an invitation.

Cartwright backed up a step and waved Ted through the door. He gestured toward chairs in front of the desk, then circled around, scratching his head, to take a seat in his swivel chair. "I sure hope what you have to say is important, Mr. Pulaski, because I have a murderer to put in jail."

"I can guarantee Lilliana is not your killer." Ted shifted in his seat, looked down at his feet, then raised his eyes and said, "I am."

"What?" Lilliana and the chief chorused. Despite Sarah's tale of an argument with Bette, Ted was the last person on earth Lilliana would have suspected of being a murderer. He was so kind, so gentle. In all the months she'd been visiting his store, she'd never seen him angry, even when faced with a particularly difficult customer. Being violent wasn't at all like him.

"I killed Bette Tesselink." Ted took out a handkerchief and wiped his brow, then sat twisting the cloth in his hands. He took a deep breath. "Lilliana told me she found out Bette was blackmailing people. I don't know why that woman took such delight in torturing the innocent. Every time you'd turn around, she was causing trouble for someone. Me included.

"I don't know how she did it, but Bette discovered something, a secret I was keeping, and threatened to go to Russ Ellison with the information. She didn't want money from me. I'm not sure what she wanted. Maybe power. Maybe something I had no desire to give her." He coughed as if his throat were dry. "Could I have a drink of water, please?"

The chief got up from his chair, opened the door, and called out to the receptionist. "DeeDee, can you bring three bottles of water in here?"

While they waited, silent, Lilliana wondered whether Bette had been looking for romance, sex, or a marriage of convenience. She doubted Ted would be specific, even if pressed.

After DeeDee delivered the water and returned to the lobby, Chief Cartwright said, "Go on."

"That day at the flower show I tried talking to her at her table, but she didn't want anyone to overhear what she had to say. She suggested we meet back in the storage room later on. I waited back there quite a while before she showed up.

"I asked her what she wanted in return for keeping my secret, but she said she'd changed her mind. She figured out the information was more valuable than anything I could offer her. She told me she was going to Ellison with it. In return, she was sure he'd let her live rent-free in the casita for life. With maybe a cut of the proceeds to boot. I told her she couldn't do that; it was wrong to exploit… the secret. Once word got out, it would never be the same. And the thing that made it so precious would disappear."

Secret? What secret could Ted have that he thought he had to kill to protect?

"She kept insisting there was no point in trying to negotiate. Her mind was made up.

"I didn't know what to do. I couldn't bear the idea of… Anyway, I lost it. I saw the bat sticking out of the equipment bag, and I grabbed it and hit her over the head. I didn't mean to kill her. I was so scared. I wiped the handle of the bat with my handkerchief and scooted out of there."

He turned to Lilliana. "That's why I didn't come back for my plant on Sunday. I wanted to stay as far away from the crime scene as possible."

"But what were you so desperate to keep Bette from talking about?" Lilliana asked.

Ted curled his upper lip over his teeth and chewed on his mustache. He scrutinized first the chief, then Lilliana, then the chief again. "It's not something I can describe in words. To really understand it, I'll have to show you. But you have to promise not to tell anyone."

That wasn't a problem for Lilliana. She trusted that if Ted said it must be kept secret, he had a good reason. "I promise."

The two of them stared at the chief. Cartwright was quiet for so long, Lilliana began to wonder if he'd lost the ability to speak. Finally he said, "I promise. As long as it's not something that's against the law."

"Oh, I can guarantee it's not," Ted said.

"Well, then, where is this big secret?" the chief of police asked.

Ted stood up and said, "Follow me."

CHAPTER TWENTY-ONE

Once they exited Town Hall, Chief Cartwright headed for his patrol car. Ted stopped him.

"You can't drive there. We have to walk. And crawl a little. It's not worth taking the car a block only to have to park it."

"Crawl?" Lilliana looked down at her clothes. While dressed in clothes a bit more stylish than she would be for a walk because of her lunch with Ted, she supposed her outfit would do for crawling. She was due for a trip to the laundry room anyway.

"What do you mean, crawl?" Chief Cartwright chimed in. He wore, of course, a uniform. From the sharpness of the creases and its immaculate condition, he had his clothes dry cleaned or laundered for him.

"You'll understand when we get there." Ted started down School Street.

The chief gave Lilliana a look as if to say 'crazy old coot,' then shrugged and followed Ted. Lilliana joined him.

For a ninety-year-old man, Ted set a brisk pace. She could

barely keep up with him, while the chief was soon huffing and puffing. Ted turned north on Canyon toward Main Street. At the corner he said, "Wait here a minute while I get some things from the store."

"Oh, no you don't," Chief Cartwright said. "I'm not going to let a confessed murderer run off by himself."

"If you really want to..." Ted appeared to be in a hurry. "Well, come along then. I have no intention of running off, as you put it. But we'll need a few things for where we're going."

The three of them traipsed to the grocery. Ted went in the back and returned bearing a couple of flashlights, a coil of rope, and a knapsack. He put the flashlights and the rope in the knapsack and hoisted the pack to his back. "Okay, let's go."

Ted led them back down Main, about fifty paces beyond the intersection with Canyon, before turning to cross the street. On this side of Canyon, there was nothing but desert in front of them and a view of the church steeple behind them. Even if it were not vacant, they wouldn't be visible from the shop on the corner opposite the grocery. Or anywhere else, as best as Lilliana could determine. Still, Ted glanced back furtively before leading them across the street. There was no traffic this time of day.

The landscape remained the same on the north side of Main Street: desert, cactus, and mesquite. But Ted obviously knew where he was going, because he didn't hesitate. He struck off into the desert and headed northwest, Lilliana and Chief Cartwright following. Within thirty paces, it became obvious they were following some kind of trail. Ted must have come this way many times before.

The rocky ground sloped uphill, making conversation

difficult as they concentrated on where they put their feet. Anyway, Ted had made it clear he wasn't going to tell them where they were going or what they would see before they actually arrived at their destination.

Lilliana soon realized they were ascending into the hills close to where she had been a couple of days ago. Her conclusion was confirmed when she heard the tinkle of flowing water and, a few minutes later, stepped out of the brush onto the bank of the stream. Ted stopped a minute to let the chief catch up. Even Lilliana was breathing heavily from the exertion.

"We should have brought some water," she said. Her dry mouth reminded her how easily dehydration could sneak up on you in Arizona. She hoped they wouldn't have to resort to drinking from the stream. The thought of drinking water the javelinas had tromped through turned her stomach.

"Oh, sorry. I did." Ted took off the pack and opened it. He reached inside and pulled out a bottle of water and handed it to her. "Do you want some, Chief?"

Chief Cartwright halted beside them, red-faced and panting. He held out a hand and gasped, "Thanks." Opening the bottle, he slugged down a good third of the water before stopping to catch his breath. "I'd better start going to the gym." He smiled weakly.

"What gym?" Lilliana asked, curious. Maybe she could join the gym to get more exercise.

"Uh, that's the problem," Chief Cartwright said. "You have to drive into Benson for a regular gym. One of the problems with being the only cop in town is you're on call twenty-four seven. It would take me too long to get back here if there was a problem in Rainbow Ranch."

Lilliana was disappointed. Then she had a thought. "Say, chief, why don't you form a softball team? We could have games. You know, the town people against the retired people. You'd probably win most of the games."

"You're forgetting you're under arrest for murder. Not likely you'll be playing softball real soon," the chief said. "Even though your... friend... has confessed."

Ted stared incredulously at Cartwright. "Surely you don't still think Lilliana is guilty?"

"Let's just say I'm keeping my options open." The chief took another long drink of water.

Ted shook his head. "I think you'll believe me when you see what I've got to show you. Ready to continue?"

After the brief rest, Cartwright's color had returned to something resembling normal. He put the cap back on his water bottle and said, "I'm ready."

Lilliana also capped her water, although she'd only drunk about a quarter of it. When outdoors in Arizona, she found it difficult to keep a balance between avoiding dehydration and needing a bathroom. "Me, too," she said.

"Okay, then." Ted turned uphill and followed the stream. After about twenty minutes, he stopped.

"Here we are," Ted said.

"Where?" Lilliana asked. She scanned their surroundings, saw nothing but desert. The stream seemed to disappear into the hillside.

"If you've made us trek all the way out here just to see desert, I'm going to arrest you on general principles." The chief was aggravated, to say the least. He took off his cap and ran his fingers through hair damp with sweat.

Ted laughed nervously. "Not quite." He looked at Lilliana and Chief Cartwright with the same apprehension he'd shown at Town Hall. "I'm sorry to ask again, but I have to be sure. Do you both promise to keep what I'm about to show you secret?"

Lilliana nodded.

"Enough already!" Chief Cartwright said, thunderclouds gathering in his eyes. "Yes. A thousand times yes. But if you're about to show me a pot farm, I will not be bound by my answer."

Ted took a deep breath and pointed to the end of the stream. "There."

Lilliana started to feel some exasperation herself. "I don't see anything."

"We have to get closer." Ted led the way to the vegetation around the source of the water and pulled back the branch of a creosote bush.

Hidden behind the bush an opening not quite hip high and about three feet across punctured the hillside. Down the center of it, the stream trickled out, not more than six inches wide at this point.

"A hole?" Cartwright exclaimed. "We came all this way to show us a hole?"

"Not a hole," Lilliana said softly, understanding for the first time. "A cave." She felt a surge of anticipation. A hidden cave to explore. Who would have guessed it?

Relief showed in Ted's face at her comprehension. "Yes, a cave. A magnificent cave."

The chief tilted his head and pursed his lips.

"You have to see the cave for yourself to understand how precious it is," Ted said. "Unfortunately, we're going to get a little muddy crawling inside. But don't worry, it widens out pretty fast into an area where we can stand up."

He waited for that to sink in and then asked, "Ready?"

"Absolutely," Lilliana said. She knelt down near the entrance and started to crawl in, but Ted put a hand on her shoulder and pressed her back.

"Let me lead the way," he said. He took off the pack again and pulled out the flashlights, handing one to Lilliana and taking the other himself. He also pulled out a yellow hard hat with a light on the front. After clipping the flashlight to his belt and putting on the hard hat, he put the pack back on and knelt beside her. He lit the lamp on his helmet and crawled inside the hole.

It was impossible for Lilliana to crawl with the flashlight in her hand, so she stuck it in her waistband and followed after Ted. The interior was incredibly dark after the bright Arizona sunshine. At first all Lilliana could see was the beam coming from the light on Ted's helmet.

They kept as far to the side of the passage as possible, but Lilliana still felt dampness on her knees as they crawled across the muddy ground. The chief grunted behind her as he brought up the rear.

Gradually her eyes adapted to the darkness. She still couldn't see much, but she felt more comfortable about going ahead in the gloom. She could hear water dripping as well as the sound of the stream running out into the world. The cave smelled of damp earth and things she couldn't identify. At least she didn't detect the stink of ammonia from bat guano, something with which she was familiar from going to Colossal Cave near Tucson.

She felt rather than saw the closeness of the walls and realized why cavers were always so thin. The morbidly obese wouldn't stand a chance of getting through this section. Even thin cavers sometimes got stuck in the tiny passages, like the famous Floyd Collins in Kentucky. She hoped Chief Cartwright, who had a bit of a donut-paunch, wasn't having any trouble.

Whatever sixth sense had told her about the closeness of the walls now told her they were getting farther away. She breathed easier, as if the walls had exerted a pressure on the air itself. Just ahead she saw the silhouette of Ted's torso as he rose to his knees. He edged forward another couple of feet, then stood up. He turned around so the light from his headlamp flooded the passage, and Lilliana could see clearly for the first time.

She had to crawl close to where Ted stood before the ceiling rose high enough for her to stand as well. They stood silently waiting for the chief to catch up. He was winded from the crawl when he arrived and stood with a sigh of relief.

Ted turned slowly, dramatically, so that his lamp now illuminated a small room, approximately eight feet in diameter and as many feet high. Red-tinged stalactites hung from the ceiling, glistening from the water that slowly dripped down their sides to the muddy floor below.

"Turn on your flashlight, Lilliana," he said. "Shine it around the room so you can enjoy the beauty here."

She did as Ted asked and was struck dumb by the glory that surrounded her. Formations in all shades of pink, some verging on red, some almost white, shone like jewels in the darkness.

"What makes them red?" she whispered, in respect for the

cathedral-like space in which they stood.

"Iron oxide," Ted said. "There must be an iron deposit, or at least iron-rich soil, above us. Rain water and snow melt drip through the iron and carry it to the limestone below. As the limestone dissolves, it picks up the iron ore."

"It's beautiful," Lilliana said.

Even Chief Cartwright was looking at their surroundings in awe. But he quickly recovered. "Okay, so it's a cave. A pretty cave," he amended. "But what makes it different from all the other caves in Arizona?"

"Ever been to Colossal Cave?" Ted asked.

"Yeah, sure," the chief replied.

"Ever seen any water there?"

The chief thought a minute and said, "No."

"Most caves, especially most commercial caves, are dry caves. They're dead. The formations stopped growing in them thousands of years ago when the water dried up. This cave is alive and growing. It's like Kartchner Caverns down south of Benson. A live cave is very rare. To have two so close together…" Ted's voice trailed off.

"So what's the big deal about keeping it a secret?" the chief asked.

Lilliana had read the story of Kartchner Caverns, so she knew the reason, but she let Ted tell the chief.

"Caves are actually very fragile environments. It takes thousands of years for a stalactite to grow. And seconds for a human being to break it off as a souvenir. There are some caves where almost all the formations were broken off by tourists or even cavers, who should know better. The two men who discovered Kartchner Caverns worked hard at keeping it a secret until they developed a plan to conserve the cave. But, even with the best intentions, the environment of Kartchner Caverns has been changed by the construction and the tours going through. There's great concern over its future."

Chief Cartwright craned his neck as he looked around the cave room. Once he'd surveyed as much as he could see, he said, "I've been to Kartchner Caverns. This little cave ain't no Kartchner."

Ted laughed. "Oh, this is just the beginning. We haven't even seen a tenth of the cave yet."

"Can we see some more?" she asked.

"Sure. There's a passage back there." Ted pointed toward an area shrouded in shadows at the back of the room. "Follow me. But be careful to walk in my footsteps so we don't damage the cave any more than it already is."

When they got closer, Lilliana could see the crevice in the back wall. Taking a clue from Ted, she ducked as she went through. The chief, being shorter and wider, didn't have to duck, but he did turn sideways so he could squeeze through. He grunted as a sharp protrusion scraped across his belly.

Ted pulled the flashlight from his belt and sent a beam of light out into the darkness. The light slid over huge stalagmites in the near distance and disappeared into the gloom beyond. When Ted turned the light toward the ceiling, hundreds, maybe thousands, of stalactites hung overhead. Lilliana turned her flashlight so its beam accompanied Ted's as it swept the room.

"How big is this place?" she asked.

"I'm not sure," Ted said. "I've never measured it. It must be at least as big as the Big Room over at Kartchner."

"Is there more?" Lilliana asked.

"Oh, there's much more," Ted said. He shone the light on the floor of the cave. It wasn't so much a floor as a jumble of boulders and limestone formations. He pointed the flashlight toward a spot a few feet from where they stood. Footprints led off into the darkness. "If you're careful, there's a sort of path through here. Are you game to try it?"

Lilliana nodded before remembering Ted probably couldn't see her. "Oh, yes!" She was entranced by the cave. A cave where no other humans had trod. While she'd always been drawn to show caves and toured many of them, they were nothing like the raw beauty of this place. This place. "Does it have a name?"

"What? Oh, you mean the cave. Well, it does, at least in my mind, but I'm going to wait a while before I tell you what it is." He was smiling, and a twinkle danced in his eyes. He was teasing her.

She kind of liked it, so she played along.

"If you two are finished flirting with one another, can we get this over with?"

She'd almost forgotten the chief was there. She was disappointed in the tone of his voice. Apparently he wasn't quite as impressed as she was with the cave.

"Of course," Ted said.

The light was too dim for her to be sure, but Lilliana thought he was blushing. From the warmth in her cheeks, she was, too.

Ted started off down the trail. Lilliana was careful to remember his instructions to step in his footprints. The chief brought up the rear. With her flashlight focused on the ground, it was hard to see any of the formations that must surround them. She heard the trickle of water just before Ted stopped and turned to face her. "Be careful here. There's water flowing over the path, and you don't want to slip."

Lilliana had been hugging the wall on her right, often reaching out to touch it for reassurance, but she edged closer to it when Ted pointed his flashlight down and to the left. Just a couple of feet away the water streamed over the edge of a precipice, a tiny waterfall splashing down into the depths of the cave. The chief looked apprehensive.

"Are you sure this is safe?" Cartwright asked.

"Just go slow, stay to the right, and plant your feet firmly before taking each step," Ted said.

It sounded like a lot of instructions to her, but most of them were intuitive. She had no intention of getting close to the slippery edge. Ted turned and resumed his journey on the path. Lilliana followed, careful of a jagged piece of rock that jutted out from the wall about waist high.

Apparently the chief hadn't seen the protrusion as he cursed and then cried out. Lilliana spun around and almost lost her balance as her feet slid on the slick surface. A thumping sound and a whoof of air was followed by another scream.

In the beam of her flashlight, Chief Cartwright peered at them from over the edge, one hand wrapped around a stalagmite, the other frantically grasping at the slippery rock. The whites of his eyes stood out in the darkness, and his face was filled with terror.

CHAPTER TWENTY-TWO

"Hold on!" Ted shouted.

Somewhat unnecessarily, in Lilliana's opinion. The chief was already holding on for all he was worth.

"Lilliana, move toward me. But stay close to the wall."

She nodded and turned her back to the wall, giving Ted as much room as possible to get past her. She stretched her arms out and felt the irregular surface with her fingers, inched her way forward. Ted brushed against her as he moved back toward the chief. He took off the backpack, knelt down, and opened it. He pulled out the length of rope he'd packed and made a lasso at one end. His life as a cowboy was going to come in handy.

"I'm going to put this rope around you," Ted said as he held up the lasso. "First under this hand—"he nodded toward the one clutching the edge"—and then I'm going to loop it around you by holding your other hand." He tilted his head toward the hand that grasped the stalagmite. His voice was as calm as the surface of the now-distant pond. It didn't hold a trace of the panic Lilliana felt threatening to burst from her in a nervous laugh or scream. She unconsciously raised her hand and covered her mouth.

The chief nodded, indicating he understood.

"Can I help?" Lilliana asked.

Ted looked over his shoulder at her. "No. I don't want you slipping over the edge, too."

Ted grasped the chief's wrist firmly and raised it barely enough to slide the rope underneath. Once that was accomplished, he lowered the chief's hand back to the ground. Lilliana crept closer. Despite the danger, she wanted to see what was happening.

Ted held the noose up in the air and slid the rope up the chief's body and over his head. The chief's right hand slipped a little bit on the damp surface, and Lilliana hoped he could hang on just a few more seconds. Ted wrapped his hand around the chief's left hand, the one that grasped the stalagmite, and paused.

"Ready?" Ted asked.

"Yeah," the chief said, although he didn't look at all sure.

As soon as Ted pulled the chief's hand away from the stalagmite, the hand clutching the edge of the precipice slipped farther. Lilliana darted forward and grabbed for it as Ted rapidly looped the rope under the chief's other hand. The pull from the weight of the chief's body was strong, and Lilliana wasn't sure she could hold on, but she heard the snap of the lasso being jerked tight around the chief. The weight threatening to pull her arm out of its socket lessened.

Ted rose to his feet, the strain of supporting Chadwick's weight etched on his face, the muscles of his arms bulging with the effort. Slowly he backed up, hauling the chief away from disaster. Lilliana added her strength as best she could while Ted pulled the chief upwards. Once he was high enough, Cartwright released his grip on the stalactite and pushed himself higher. Finally he flopped his body back on the trail, and Lilliana let out her held breath. The chief panted from the exertion. Or perhaps it was fear. Even Ted's face looked a little gray in the lamplight.

Once the chief caught his breath, he looked up at Ted from his prone position and said, "Thanks." Then he turned toward Lilliana. "You, too, Mrs. Wentworth."

"Maybe we should turn back," Lilliana said. She'd been shaken by how close the chief had been to falling and possibly dying.

"It's only a few more steps until we're off this ledge and into another room," Ted said. "We can catch our breath there before navigating our way back."

"I suppose it's up to the chief," Lilliana said.

Cartwright sat up and wrapped his hands around his knees. His color was a little better, and his voice took on a false bravado. "I say we go ahead. It was my fault I went over the edge. I tried to see how deep it was and leaned over too far. From now on, I'll stay close to the wall."

Lilliana doubted the truthfulness of his statement. The chief was probably too embarrassed to admit how afraid he'd been. The easiest way for him to prove his bravery would be to insist they continue. But she didn't want to challenge his manhood. "Very well." She turned to Ted. "Lead on, MacDuff!"

Ted was true to his word. In fewer than ten steps the ledge opened out onto a platform overlooking another largish room of the cave. "Shine your light here," Ted said, indicating the direction with the beam from his own flashlight.

Lilliana's light joined Ted's in illuminating a tremendous column of limestone, a feature where a stalagmite and a stalactite had met eons ago and joined. It must have been three feet in diameter, with traceries of smaller stalactites flowing down its sides like icicles.

"It's beautiful," she said, in awe at the mammoth structure.

"It is pretty, isn't it?" the chief agreed.

"Turn your light on the ceiling," Ted said as he completed the action he'd instructed Lilliana to take.

She gasped. Overhead thousands of delicate structures not only hung from the ceiling, but twisted and turned in defiance of gravity in patterns like frost on a window.

"Those are called helictites," Ted said as he played his light over them so they sparkled.

"It's like a fairyland," Cartwright said, finally appreciating the uniqueness of the cave.

Ted started, then recovered. "Yes, it is." He turned to Lilliana. "You were asking what the name of the cave was." He glanced up at the ceiling. "I call it Fairyland."

"And no wonder," she said. "It's the perfect name for this place."

"In more ways than one," Ted said softly.

Lilliana gave him a sharp stare. "What do you mean?"

"There's another passage up ahead. With all I've shown you, I think you can understand why I was so anxious to keep the cave secret."

"I get it now," the chief said. "If people knew about it, this cave might become as big an attraction as Kartchner Caverns.

Probably have all kinds of government people involved, too. Pretty soon, Rainbow Ranch wouldn't be the nice, quiet town it is today. That wouldn't sit well with the people who live here."

"Those were my thoughts, too," Ted said. "We have to protect the town as well as the cave."

"And Bette was going to ruin both," Lilliana said.

Ted nodded. "She thought she could get Ellison to put up the money for the development of the cave. She was counting on a share of the profits for herself." He took a deep breath. "But there's more. Much more. What I'm going to show you at the end of the next passage really can't be shared with anyone." He waited for their agreement.

Lilliana nodded back at him.

"How much farther do we need to go? And how big is that passage?" the chief asked.

"Oh, maybe thirty-forty yards," Ted said. "The trail there isn't quite as wet as the one we came over to get here."

"You know, I think I've seen enough," the chief said. "Why don't the two of you go ahead. I'll wait here where there's a big, flat space for me to stand on."

"You're sure you won't mind being alone?" Ted asked.

The chief shook his head. "Not as long as you leave me one of those flashlights. And don't dawdle too long."

Ted handed the chief his flashlight. "Just yell if you need us. Sound carries pretty good in here."

"I'll be fine."

"Ready, Lilliana?" Ted asked. He held out his hand to her.

"I'm ready," she replied as she took his hand.

CHAPTER TWENTY-THREE

They stepped off into the darkness, Ted leading the way, his headlight beam shining just far enough ahead of them to see the path. The only sounds were the drip of water and the pad of their footsteps. Something about the intimacy of the darkness kept her from speaking. Ted must have felt it, too, because it was a long time before he said anything.

"We're coming to another narrow spot." His voice was quiet, almost a whisper. "Follow me and you should have plenty of room."

"All right," Lilliana whispered back.

They continued in silence as they squeezed through the gap in the limestone wall. Lilliana felt rather than saw the space widen around them at the end of the passage. Ted stopped and Lilliana stepped up beside him.

"I'm kind of glad the chief didn't come with us," Ted said.

"Oh?" It was too late if Cartwright decided to tell the world about the secret of the cave. He'd already been shown enough of it to realize its commercial value.

Ted looked bashful. "Uh, because he might not believe his eyes. And, if he did, he probably wouldn't be able to keep quiet about what I'm going to show you next."

"What might that be?" asked Lilliana. She couldn't think of anything that would be more impressive than what she'd already seen.

"The real reason I call this place Fairyland."

It couldn't be, she thought, but before she could ask for an explanation, Ted trotted out into this new room. Lilliana had to hurry to keep up with him, and she barely caught glances of their surroundings as they rushed through the inky chamber. Even so, the stalactites and stalagmites she glimpsed on either side were amazing. They passed by curtains of stone, striated red and white, that resembled nothing so much as slices of bacon, and several columns almost as big as the one they'd seen in the big room. Now they were circling around a huge limestone formation shaped like a warrior's shield. As they emerged on the other side, Lilliana saw an oval chamber, egg-like in its dimensions, the inside of it covered in those amazing helictites growing in multiple directions and sparkling in the light of Ted's lamp. She raised her flashlight in order to better examine the formations.

"Lower your light," Ted hissed.

Startled, she did as he asked.

"Sorry," Ted said. "But you need to keep the light down below eye level." He turned and swept his hand toward a niche in the wall at about the same height as their eyes. The helictites crusting the niche glowed with a soft light of their own. Bioluminescence? Sunlight through a crack from the world above? Or magic?

"This," he said, "is Queen Esmeralda."

Lilliana blinked to clear her vision. What she was seeing couldn't be possible. It must be a trick of the light, or some odd mold, or a bird trapped inside the cave. She'd made that mistake once before, she thought. *Or had she?* No matter how many times she blinked her eyes, the vision didn't change. Seated on a purple silk pillow covering the top of a small stalagmite was a fairy.

The fairy couldn't have been more than six inches tall when standing. She had large, purple, butterfly wings which she waved slowly back and forth. She wore something like a ballet costume, white tights with a bustier that left her shoulders exposed, and a gossamer skirt over all.

Lilliana looked at Ted, hoping for confirmation this was real. He nodded.

"I am pleased to meet you, Queen Esmeralda," she said. She extended a finger to shake hands with the fairy, then wondered if she shouldn't bow instead.

Esmeralda touched her finger, graciously showing she was not offended by the gesture. "And I you, Lilliana. Ted has told me so much about you."

"You have?" Lilliana asked Ted, her eyes wide.

"Yes, I have." Ted was smiling. "I needed to let Esmeralda know that you might reach the cave in your exploring. Most of the time the fairies put a light glamour over the entrance so it isn't discovered by accident, but you're so persistent and discerning, I thought you might be able to see through the glamour."

"'They are fairies; he that speaks to them shall die. I'll wink and couch; no man their works must eye,'" Lilliana quoted from *The Merry Wives of Windsor*. Realizing what the quote meant, she said with alarm, "I hope we won't die."

Ted chuckled. "If it were death to speak to fairies, I'd be long gone."

Lilliana relaxed at the reassurance. Then she realized what Ted had said. "Fairies? Are there more than one?"

"Yes, there are." Esmeralda smiled at her. "We thought it would be best if you met me first. If anything untoward happened, the rest of my court would still be safe."

"I would never hurt you," Lilliana said.

"That's clear now." The queen of the fairies raised her voice and called out. "Come out, Goodly People, and meet our guest."

From behind the stalagmite where the queen sat, a fairy, this one arrayed in yellow, appeared and moved to the queen's right. After her came another, a little man, dressed in green tights, who stood on the queen's left. Another lady, dressed in cerulean blue, appeared and joined the fairy in yellow. Eventually there were a dozen fairies, six standing on either side of the queen, a cacophony of color amid the black and shades of gray of the cave.

"How delightful!" Lilliana exclaimed. "I am so happy to meet you all."

The fairy court bowed to her in response.

"But why are they living in a cave?" she asked Ted. "And how is it that no one but you has seen them?"

"That's not quite true," Esmeralda said. "I believe you've seen Buidheag-an-t-Samhraidh, Buttercup you would call her." She indicated the yellow fairy, who curtseyed and lowered her head.

"So I wasn't imagining things," Lilliana said.

Esmeralda smiled. "No, you weren't. I had to warn Buidheag to be more careful when she goes outside."

Ted sighed. "It's hard for them to find a place of safety in our modern age. In the old country—England, Scotland, and Ireland—they lived in the forests and sometimes beneath hills. I'm not sure how this band came to be in Arizona—even Esmeralda doesn't know—but we have few forests, and the hills aren't the soft loam of the British Isles. So when they found this cave with the stream nearby, it looked the most like home they'd seen in the New World."

Lilliana felt sad for the fairies and turned a commiserating gaze on Esmeralda.

"Don't feel sad for us," Esmeralda said as if reading her mind. "This place is very beautiful. And we do get to go outside you know. We even visit some of you while you're asleep."

"What..." Lilliana began to say. She couldn't believe the fairies dared to approach humans, even sleeping ones.

Ted had a smile on his face. "Don't tell me you haven't noticed little gifts left for you?"

She thought of her lost button and the wafers Willie found that suppressed his appetite. "Why, I suppose I have."

"The fairies like doing that. They also have a mischievous streak, so you might want to be careful with some of their gifts. One time they left me a pretty flower. I lifted it to my nose to smell it and couldn't stop sneezing for hours."

The tinkle of fairy laughter filled the cave. Lilliana was glad they were too small to deliver items of real damage—say, a rat trap in place of her alarm clock.

"Hallllloooooo." The cry echoed down the cavern.

"It sounds like the chief is getting tired of being alone," Ted said. "We'd better get back to him before he tries to follow us here."

"You're right," Lilliana said. "It's been wonderful meeting you, Your Majesty."

"And I, you," Esmeralda said. "Please come back and visit."

"Oh, I will," Lilliana said. "I'd love to come back with Ted to visit you."

"Good-bye, Esmeralda," Ted said.

The fairy queen gazed at him adoringly. "Good-bye, dear friend."

* * *

"About time you got back," the chief groused. "What took you so long?"

"We found some interesting formations to look at," Lilliana said. "We lost track of the time."

"Well, it's getting cold in here," the chief said. "I'm ready to get back to the sunlight."

"I think we all are," Ted agreed.

The three of them made their way back to the cave exit without any further incidents. The chief navigated the narrow, wet trail easily this time. Despite all the beauty Lilliana had seen inside, she was relieved to emerge into daylight at the end of their trek.

Cartwright sighed audibly as he stood up and attempted to brush the dirt and mud from his uniform. He made a face. "Guess I'm going to have to get this dry cleaned again."

"But wasn't it worth it?" Lilliana asked.

"I guess," the chief said begrudgingly.

"Why don't we sit here for a minute?" Ted said. "I brought some sandwiches along. I don't know about the two of you, but I'm hungry."

"Me, too." The chief looked much more cheerful at the prospect of food.

The three of them were already so dirty, no one objected to sitting on the ground by the bank of the stream. Ted pulled thick sandwiches from his pack and handed one to each of them.

Much to her surprise, Lilliana was ravenous. She'd eaten half her sandwich before she paused and took note of her surroundings. Now that they had seen what Ted had been keeping secret, she understood his motivation to kill Bette. Kind of. She doubted she'd do the same, but was glad she hadn't been forced to make the choice.

"I suppose you'll still have to arrest Ted," she said regretfully. She didn't want Ted to go to jail, perhaps face the death penalty, but murder couldn't go unpunished.

"That's right," Chief Cartwright said. "It appears I was wrong about you, Mrs. Wentworth."

She waved her hand, brushing away his concern. "Understandable under the circumstances. But next time, you might want to wait for all the evidence before you arrest someone."

The chief nodded.

Ted was quiet. He hadn't eaten much of his sandwich. From what Lilliana had seen before, this wasn't like him. He raised a hand to his chest.

"Are you all right?" she asked.

"I'm fine. Just a little heartburn is all." He smiled wanly. "I should have brought some Rolaids with me."

Unlike Ted, the chief had finished all of his sandwich and was licking his fingers. While they'd eaten, the sun had slipped lower in the sky. Twilight was approaching. "Should we start back?" Lilliana asked.

"Yep," the chief said. "I've still got a lot of paperwork to do. And it looks like I'll be driving into Bisbee after all, only not with you, Mrs. Wentworth."

The three of them rose and headed down the path leading back to town. Ted walked slower than he had all day. Although they'd certainly had their share of exercise exploring the cave, Lilliana had never seen him slow down before. His lips were tight, and every once in a while, he grimaced. She was worried about him.

The sky was getting darker. The three of them reached Main Street just about the time of the evening rush hour. For a change, there were actually cars speeding down the road, commuters from Benson and Bisbee on their way home. Headlights appeared from the south, approached, then passed on up to the north and east residential areas. Lilliana paused at the edge of the road in an abundance of caution, waiting for the lights that had just appeared to pass. Cartwright waited beside her.

For some reason, Ted didn't wait. He dashed across Main Street as if there was some kind of emergency, a sprint when he'd been walking so slowly all the way back. When he reached the other side, he stopped and clutched at his chest.

Lilliana darted out ahead of an approaching car and raced toward him. Horns blared and tires squealed as cars swerved to avoid hitting her, but she didn't care. Fear for Ted overrode any thought of safety. Before Lilliana could reach him, Ted collapsed to the ground.

Running the last few feet, she arrived at Ted's prostrate form. She crouched beside him, begged him to speak to her, tears cascading down her face. In seconds Cartwright caught up and knelt next to her. He took Ted's pulse, then shook his head.

"No!" Lilliana wailed. Moments ago, she'd been dismayed at the thought of Ted going to jail. She would have gladly traded jail for this horrible alternative. The warm, gentle man she'd only begun to know was dead.

"Sorry, Mrs. Wentworth. It must have been a heart attack. Man of his age, and what he did, it's not unusual." He pulled out his phone and called for an ambulance. In less than fifteen minutes the volunteer crew of EMTs arrived at the scene, but there was nothing they could do except transport the body.

CHAPTER TWENTY-FOUR

Out on her patio, Lilliana worked on repotting several of her African violets. Repotting them, watering them, grooming them, and generally caring for her plants eased her pain. In part she was proving to herself that she could keep things she held dear alive. A tear traced down her cheek.

Chief Cartwright had decided that, with her as witness to Ted's statement, he could close the case of Bette Tesselink's murder. They agreed not to specify what the secret was she threatened to reveal. With the evidence Lilliana had gathered about her other blackmail victims, disclosing the secret hadn't seemed necessary. Or wise.

Lilliana had walked by Bette's casita one day, found Miguel carrying out half-used cleaning supplies and toilet paper rolls and assorted linens, and dumping them in a cart to throw away. Susan had done the same thing most people did when they abandoned a rental property. She took away the things she thought of value, left behind those she didn't care to keep.

Recognizing the table cloths, Lilliana dug in among them as

soon as Miguel turned his back. She found the japanned box, the one with the keyhole to match the size of the little key. She couldn't wait to get the box back to her apartment and open it.

Inside she found a small notebook. Each page had a name at the top, with a list of dates and dollar amounts beneath it. So many people had been Bette's victims.

Lilliana waited to make sure Cartwright closed the murder case, then tore out each page and put it through her shredder. She kept the box.

She thought the chief would keep the secret of the cave, but she'd keep her ears open for any murmurs about it in town. And hoped no one would find out about the fairies.

She put down the newest True Blue cultivar she'd started from a leaf of the original plant and hoped it would bloom true. You couldn't always count on that. So many people had come to her wanting a True Blue African violet, whether because it was so pretty or because of the connection to Bette she didn't know. She was sure she could sell as many as she could raise at the fall sale.

She picked up the next pot and put a wet strand of yarn through the hole in the bottom of it before spooning in a layer of perlite. She added some loose, moist soil, then poked a small hole. Lilliana picked up the next leaf she'd gathered from the mature hybrid and sliced off the stem at an angle before putting it in the hole. After shaking the pot gently to settle the soil, she tamped it down oh-so-lightly to make sure the leaf would stay in place. One more done.

She'd lost so many in her life over the past couple of years. Although she'd known Ted was ninety, he never acted like it. The man was so vigorous, always moving, stocking the grocery, walking between his home and the store.

The ME confirmed that he'd had a heart attack. She'd seen no hint of a heart condition until their trip to the cave. Ted had been surprisingly healthy despite his age, but apparently not all his arteries shared that good health.

She wondered what might have happened between them if Ted hadn't died. There was no way to tell, of course, but she'd felt a connection from the first time they'd met. When he shared the secret only known to himself, she felt that connection deepen. Now she'd never know what might have been.

She wondered who—if anyone—would take over Pulaski's Gourmet Grocery. If it didn't reopen, she would have to order her Earl Grey tea online—maybe from Amazon. There was irony in that thought. A very traditional, almost old-fashioned tea from the largest Internet retailer. And wherever would she get those chocolates Ted stocked near the cash register?

She put the last pot down and rubbed her hands together to scrub off most of the dirt. There. Six more plants to sell. She picked up two of them to carry down to her guest bathroom to nurture.

There wasn't much room left in the bathroom. She'd started so many plants in the last week, tiny pots covered almost all the horizontal surfaces. She barely squeezed the two she was holding onto the shelf over the toilet tank.

As she exited the bathroom, her eyes paused on the door across the hall. Crossing to it, she paused and placed her palm on the door, feeling for the presence she'd tried to preserve. She took a deep breath and opened it.

The room was exactly the same as the day Charles died. The

big hospital bed near the window so he could look outside. The get well cards on the dresser. Lilliana hadn't been able to bring herself to even pack up Charles's clothes. All of them hung in the closet.

She'd been waiting to see if Charles was still here.

She thought of how Frank had turned his bedroom into a plant room. This room was about the same size, and the window let in lots of light. She'd be able to have an indoor potting table. And grow lots more plants.

She stood quiet, listening, breathing. Charles wasn't here. He was with Ted and all the others who had passed on before. Had been for almost a year. Hopefully, they'd all be waiting for her when she joined them in heaven.

Meanwhile, she had African violets to grow.

* * *

Keep reading to find out what mystery Lilliana solves next! Turn the page for Chapter One of BLOOD RED MURDER!

There's nothing better than a good mystery. To me, solving the puzzles and seeing justice done are what mysteries are all about. I loved meeting Lilliana and her friends. I hope you did, too. If you liked this book, please leave a review now.

Join Elise's newsletter for deals, sneak peeks, and more.

THANK YOU!

Thank you for reading *True Blue Murder!* I hope you enjoyed it. If you liked it, please consider leaving a review or rating on the site where it was purchased. Reviews on Goodreads are always appreciated. Your help in spreading the word is gratefully appreciated and reviews make a huge difference to helping new readers find the series.

Get your free bonus story!

See how Lilliana solves "The Case of the Silver Scorpion." You will also be notified of new releases, giveaways, and pre-release specials by signing up for my newsletter at https://elisemstoneauthor.com/newsletter/.

Books in the Rainbow Ranch mystery series:
Homicide on the Range
Bury Me Not

Books in the African Violet Club mystery series:
True Blue Murder
Blood Red Murder
Royal Purple Murder
Double Pink Murder
Ghost White Murder

Holly Green Murder

Books in the Shipwreck Point mystery series:
The Case of the Mysterious Madam
The Case of the Angry Artist
The Case of the Comely Clairvoyant
The Case of the Seafaring Santa
The Case of the Troubled Tycoon
The Case of the Pirate's Puzzle

If you like police procedurals, try my Lacy Davenport Mystery Shorts:
Murder at the Museum
Murder in Stella Mann

ABOUT THE AUTHOR

Elise M. Stone was born and raised in New York, went to college in Michigan, lived in the Boston area for eight years, and not too long ago moved to sunny Tucson, Arizona, where she doesn't have to shovel snow. Her first degree was in psychology, her second in computers. She's worked as a pizza maker, library clerk, waitress, social worker, programmer, and data jockey.

She wrote her first story in kindergarten. She loved writing stories.

Now that she's retired from her job as a computer programmer, she once again is writing stories. She hopes you enjoy them.

I love hearing from readers. You can connect with me at:
Email: elisemstone@gmail.com
Twitter: @EliseMStone
Facebook: www.facebook.com/EliseMStone

ACKNOWLEDGMENTS

No one writes a book totally on their own. While I tend to be more independent than most, rarely showing my fiction to anyone until it's been through at least one complete revision, even I need another set of eyes to see things I miss.

For "True Blue Murder," Judith Ann Horner provided those eyes. She brought her own perspective to the work and helped me make this into a better story. She graciously volunteered their time and effort and willingly met my insane timetable.

The beautiful and perfectly appropriate new cover was designed by Susan Coils of Coverkicks. San took my vague ideas and turned them into an eye-catching design.

I also want to thank the Tucson Chapter of Sisters in Crime for their support and encouragement. Long before I felt worthy of calling myself a writer, they added "Author" to my membership badge and never doubted my abilities.

And last, but certainly not least, I'd like to thank all the people who have read my books. I have been overwhelmed at the response to the African Violet Club mystery series. When I started the first book as a lark during National Novel Writing Month, I never dreamed it would be published, much less enjoyed by so many people. Thank you not only for reading, but for kindly leaving reviews of the books.

Made in United States
Troutdale, OR
11/25/2023

14941192R00130